The BROO

The Case of the
HIDDEN SHOE

*TO: Gay
Well -- I did it! Wrote my first young mystery; it was so much fun! Hope you enjoy this mini "Nancy Drew" story, sis! :)
Love,
Toby A. Williams
July 26, 2021*

By Toby A. Williams

The BROOKE LYNN Mysteries
The Case of the
HIDDEN SHOE

Copyright © 2021 by Toby A Williams

Published July 2021 by Toby A\Williams
The BROOKE LYNN Adventures and Mysteries Books

All rights reserved. This book, or parts thereof, may not be reproduced in any form without written permission from the Publisher. This is a fictional middle-grade story and not based on any actual person, place, or event (living or deceased). Any resemblance is entirely coincidental.

ISBN: 978-1-7354229-1-6 (Paperback)
ISBN: 978-1-7354229-2-3 (Hardcover)

eBook available on Amazon.com

Written by *Toby A. Williams*
Cover Design/Illustration by *Corrina Holyoake*
Edited by *Calico Editing Services*

www.tobyawilliamsauthor.com

Table of Contents

Chapter One: Brooke Lynn Gale 1
Chapter Two: Ups and Downs 5
Chapter Three: Friendship Twists 9
Chapter Four: New Mike – New Bike 13
Chapter Five: What a Site! 17
Chapter Six: Mysterious Shoe 21
Chapter Seven: Puzzling Red Stains 25
Chapter Eight: New Rules 29
Chapter Nine: Big Brother 33
Chapter Ten: Pop Quiz Nightmare 37
Chapter Eleven: Balancing Act 41
Chapter Twelve: Sole Visit 45
Chapter Thirteen: Open-Minded 49
Chapter Fourteen: Who is Mr. Clemens? 53
Chapter Fifteen: Get a Clue 57
Chapter Sixteen: Mike Larkin Shares 61
Chapter Seventeen: Give and Take 67
Chapter Eighteen: Sneaking Out 71
Chapter Nineteen: Close Call or Not 75
Chapter Twenty: A Hunch 79
Chapter Twenty-One: The Announcement 83
Chapter Twenty-Two: Girlie Fun 89
Chapter Twenty-Three: Mirror-Mirror 93
Chapter Twenty-Four: Susie On Site 97
Chapter Twenty-Five: Two Sleuths and Sam 101
Chapter Twenty-Six: Could Spell Trouble 105
Chapter Twenty-Seven: Busted 109
Chapter Twenty-Eight: Grounded 113
Chapter Twenty-Nine: Room for Mom 117
Chapter Thirty: Class Speeches 119
Chapter Thirty-One: Susie Reynolds Talks 125
Chapter Thirty-Two: Ask Mike 129
Chapter Thirty-Three: Grand Opening Party 133
Chapter Thirty-Four: Surprise Client 139
Chapter Thirty-Five: It's a Wrap! 143
About the Author… 147

Books by Toby A. Williams

The BROOKE LYNN Adventures
Children's Rhyming Series

My Lil' Ladybug Friend
My Lil' Big Ocean
My Lil' First School
My Lil' New Pup
My Lil' Santa Visit

The BROOKE LYNN Mysteries
Middle-Grade Fiction Series

The Case of the Hidden Shoe

Chapter One

BROOKE LYNN GALE

She pedaled over to her best friend's house like her life depended on it… she'd know *what* to do!

Brooke Lynn raced across the front porch, her ratty sneakers scuffing the worn flagstone landing. She leaned into the doorbell again. She had texted her bestie ahead of time to be certain she'd be home!

Now, where is she?!

It felt like forever before Susie came to the door. Instantly, Brooke Lynn relaxed her clenched fists at her friend's warm smile.

Susie was dressed in a rad outfit as usual. Her sleek black ponytail drew attention to the hot pink bow. A pale green streak hung loosely by her left ear, a new addition to her locks. Unlike Brooke Lynn, every hair was in place. The girl's brown eyes widened as she took in her friend who was sweaty and rumpled after a frantic bike ride. Brooke Lynn let out a long, exasperated sigh. Susie raised both eyebrows.

"Hey, you look stressed. Come in… tell me what's up," Susie offered.

Brooke Lynn smelled the lemony scent of household cleaner when she stepped over the threshold. The neat living room looked spotless. Afraid her old sneakers would track dirt in, she looked behind to make sure she hadn't left any marks on the light grey carpet.

"Well…" Brooke Lynn said.

She didn't know where to begin, but she did know that Susie would listen. She plopped onto the over-stuffed couch and stewed.

Susie Reynolds was just like a sister, and sometimes Brooke Lynn truly wished that she *was* her sister. Then she wouldn't have to put up with her annoying older brother on her own. He was always poking fun at her.

"Why don't you act more like Susie? You can be such a baby. Grow up," her brother teased.

Although Susie had just turned 12, Brooke Lynn thought she could easily pass for 14 or 15… a real high schooler. She possessed a poise that Brooke Lynn couldn't fully grasp. Maybe it was the fact that Susie helped raise her younger brother, Jimmy. At one of their sleepovers, Susie confided about her dad's tragic death.

"My mom thought moving to Santa Mesa would be a new start after my dad's awful car wreck. It was so traumatic. We were in shock by his passing for months. It's still difficult to talk about but I can understand why my mother made the choice. Well, sort of, you know?"

Susie was only seven years old when a horrible car accident took her dad's life. Brooke Lynn guessed that sudden fatal circumstance may have contributed to her mature attitude.

Brushing aside that personal reflection, Brooke Lynn sat pouting. She realized her fists were balled up again. She picked up the fuchsia fuzzy pillow next to her and hugged it like it was a teddy bear.

"Let me guess…" Susie grinned. "It has something to do with either your brother or Mikey, right?"

"Mike," Brooke Lynn corrected. "He wants me to call him Mike now that he's 12. Mikey sounds too babyish," she mocked. "He *is* a big baby!" She let go of the pillow in disgust, then placed it back in its original spot.

"Fair enough. But what's really got you bothered?" Susie sighed.

"There's something different about Mike. Have you noticed?" Brooke Lynn asked.

Susie listened, half-thinking her friend might stomp her feet at any second. Brooke Lynn sat up and straightened her slouched shoulders.

"Um, not sure what you mean by different? How?" Susie answered.

"His babyface is gone and he's filled out. Maybe from playing summer league soccer. He's pretty lean and fit now. I don't know... I um, like he seems more confident. Besides that, he hung out with the team most of the summer. Now that we're 7th graders, he doesn't seem to want to hang out as much. It's got me so confused."

Brooke Lynn's child-like expression took on a unique look – one of defeat. Her hand reached for the bright pillow again but rubbed the fuzzy knap instead.

"Mike's been too busy with other activities that don't include me," Brooke Lynn huffed.

She wiped the spittle from her chin. Susie muzzled her giggle, not wanting to offend her friend.

"Oh that... ah ha, yes, he's gotten taller and he's cuter. A lot cuter! I couldn't pin-point what was different about him, but now that you've mentioned it, he has changed. So that's what he did all summer? Well for sure, he's not the sickly-looking kid anymore. A lot of our classmates have changed. Where have you been?" her friend replied.

She watched Brooke Lynn squirm for a minute, paying close attention to her bestie's animation. She explained things with her hands.

"I'm not talking about *that* stuff. And, silly you, it's been ages since his heart surgery. Of course, he's not sick anymore. But anyway, Susie, here's something different; when we went bike riding a few weeks ago, when Mike finally had some time for me, well, I felt self-conscious, you know? Like I was a little nervous before meeting up with him. I'm a mess... not sure what to do! It's been weighing on me for a while. I just needed to talk to you. Weird, huh?" Brooke Lynn asked.

"Yikes, Brooke Lynn! Sounds like you may have feelings for Mike, maybe more than just buddies. You've never felt uncomfortable around him before. Do you have a crush on Mikey?" Susie assumed.

Annoyed at her friend, Brooke Lynn rolled her eyes, then squinted her almond-shaped hazel eyes. She thought Susie was being so dramatic. Upset by such an assumption, Brooke Lynn fidgeted with the loose hem on her T-shirt.

"No-no, I don't… it's just that, er-um well, do you think I need a bra?"

Brooke Lynn stretched her shirt tightly around her midriff. She stuck out her chest, waiting for a reaction. Susie stifled her snickers again.

"Well, if you're self-conscious about that, I can help. You know I love shopping. For me, well, it just takes a little extra time each day to put my outfits together. Makes me feel better when I make the effort," Susie said.

Brooke Lynn did feel calmer now that she had vented to her bestie.

"This is all normal stuff, these crazy feelings around boys. It's all weird but part of getting older. I'm still trying to figure it out myself," Susie reassured Brooke Lynn.

Chapter Two

UPS AND DOWNS

Brooke Lynn secretly wished Susie would offer some of her trendy hand-me-downs. She thought maybe that would boost her self-confidence, like Susie's confidence would rub off on her.

"About a bra, well, it's probably a good idea for you to wear some coverage. Something like a camisole or bra of some type, maybe like a sports bra. Gosh, I've had to wear a bra for over a year, and I know I waited too long! I can help you if you want. Gives me an excuse to go shopping! Tell you what, talk to your mom about it first," Susie said.

Susie stared off dreaming of shopping, mentally starting a list.

Brooke Lynn had become a tad more self-conscious about what to wear each day. With just a dab of pink lip gloss, she normally felt fine about her natural appearance. Not lately, her main problem was her budding, small chest. She had avoided it long enough.

Standing a smidge above five feet tall, Brooke Lynn Gale felt average for her 11 and ¾ years old. The youngest in her class each year, she couldn't wait until she turned 12 mid-December. Other than a little stubborn baby fat lingering in a few choice places, not much concerned her… until this school year!

Brooke Lynn's phone pinged, bringing them back to reality.

"Speaking of the devil… it's Mike wondering if I want to go check out the nasty housing development tomorrow. You know the one at the far end of our neighborhood by the Oak Grove Park? I guess he's finally got time for me," Brooke Lynn said.

"K CU TOM @ 3 ☺," she texted Mike.

She had hesitated before sending, then added a smiley instead of the heart emoji. She didn't want to give him the wrong impression.

"Hey, tell Mike I said hi and I'll see him in class tomorrow," Susie pounced.

Susie's request was a biting reminder that for the first time since Kindergarten, Brooke Lynn wasn't in the same class with her friends! Letting that sink in, she sadly exhaled.

"HI FM SUSIE," she texted on the fly, cramming her phone away.

With her two closest friends getting to know each other, she hoped this would ease the knot she felt when tugged by one or the other. Maybe Mike would want to hang out more.

"Yeah, I almost forgot you two are in the same class this year. What's Mr. Clemens like?" Brooke Lynn asked.

"Hmm, let me think… okay, he's nerdy, kind of balding and skinny but very friendly. Oh, and he has these weird sideburns like that old-time singer, Elvis. But he takes time to talk one-on-one to each of us. It's the first time a teacher has been, well, personal and seems to care about our studies. Another quirky thing… he likes being called Mr. C.," Susie stated.

"I like my new teacher too. Hey, I forgot to tell you, there's this new cute boy in my class, Todd Smythe. Just moved here from Sacramento. I've seen him riding on the bike trails. He seems cool. Do you know who I mean? I was thinking about asking him to go hiking."

"Yeah, I know him and we've actually talked in the cafeteria a couple of times. I think he's cute too. I wonder if he's related to the developer guy. It says on the sign at the new housing site, Smythe Development. Like maybe his cousin or something?" Susie questioned.

"I think he said his uncle was the one building the new project. Anyway, there's a couple of cute boys in our grade this year. I just think most of them act kind of dorky. I just wish they'd grow up!"

Brooke Lynn gave a light tap to her friend's arm as she brushed by.

"Susie, I still can't believe we're in Middle School. Thanks for listening to me rant about Mike and stupid boys. I'm sure everything will be okay. Still have my chores to finish so, I guess I'd better go," Brooke Lynn said.

"Um, Brooke Lynn, is it okay if I go with you two sometime, I mean, over to the new houses? I'd like to see what all the hoopla is about. And why'd you call it nasty? Everyone is talking about the development, mostly good stuff, including my mom. I'd like to see it first-hand."

Until now, Susie hadn't shown any interest in hanging out with Mike. She didn't even like bike riding. Brooke Lynn loved exploring, riding on the bike paths, and getting dirty. She was always willing to take a good tumble on the dirt trails.

It suddenly hit her. This unexpected twist made Brooke Lynn stop in her tracks.

*Wait, does Susie **like** Mike?*

Chapter Three

FRIENDSHIP TWISTS

"Susie, really? I didn't know you cared about what was happening over there. Word's out that the developer might close off the bike trails that run through the area. Plus, I heard my mother talking about saving the oak trees in the grove. I just want to make sure nothing suspicious is going on over there."

Brooke Lynn stared at her friend with stink eye.

The Oak Grove Park area held special memories to Santa Mesa residents. The small grove of oak trees had been a family outing and recreational spot for many generations. It marked the entrance to hiking trails and bike paths around the foothills. The picnic area with wooden tables, open barbecue pits, volleyball court and even a rope swing gave that location deep-rooted meaning to the locals.

Brooke Lynn was normally happy at the thought of a new place to explore. Her cheeks grew warm like a fresh sunburn at her friend's request. She wiped away the moisture forming on her upper lip. Spending more time with Mike was what Brooke Lynn had been wanting. Her heart sank at the thought of Susie tagging along. It just felt off.

*OMG, things **are** changing but not how I wanted.*

"Well, let me check with Mike after we scope it out first. Then I'll let you know," Brooke Lynn answered.

Brooke Lynn and Mike had been best friends since they were five years old. Over time, they had become partners in crime… crime-solvers in the neighborhood. She first called him Mikey while he was recovering from heart surgery. She had visited him every day while he recuperated. When he'd asked her recently to stop calling him Mikey, the words stung. She felt sad and missed the old friendship.

*Is he pushing **me** away?*

"Yeah, Brooke Lynn, everyone's curious about it with the upcoming party and all. We just got our flyer in the mail yesterday. It's an invitation from the developer at the Oak Grove Homes. They'll have food, ice cream from Hammond's, games, face painting, even a live band. Lots of guessing going on around town about who'll be moving into the fancy new homes. They'll announce who the first homeowner will be at the party. Maybe someone famous like a movie star. That would liven up this dull town. Anyway, it's all free… so I'd love to check it out with you and Mike…" Susie trailed off.

"Geez, Susie, I said I'd let you know," Brooke Lynn snapped!

According to Susie, Santa Mesa was boring and uneventful. It was a small rural area in California just below the Central Valley. The downtown had remained unchanged since anyone could remember. Last year, Brooke Lynn's mother had confirmed its slow pace to the tweens.

"Yup, Susie, not much new going on in this sleepy town. It hasn't changed since we were your age, except Miller's Department Store. We watched every brick being laid. That was our excitement in high school. But we love it here. Lots of history too."

Her friend's stories about growing up by the coast intrigued Brooke Lynn. She had only visited the ocean a handful of times. And this inland valley was all she knew. She was fond of their quaint hub, nestled against the rolling hills. Susie didn't want to let the subject drop.

"Yeah, kind of dullsville in this town and this is the most happening thing right now. I'd like to tag along, but only if you two don't mind? Let me know," Susie pushed.

"Geez, Susie, you just don't *get it!*" Brooke Lynn exclaimed. It was like Susie couldn't care less about the developer shutting off access to the trails, chopping down the trees or taking out their picnic spot. All she was interested in was the party.

Susie's face dropped with disappointment. Brooke Lynn knew she had hurt her friend's feelings with the abrupt remark.

She can be so irritating sometimes.

Brooke Lynn lightened up before speaking again.

"Sorry, it's just that I'll have to double-check with Mike first to see what his schedule looks like. And I'll ask my mom about shopping, okay? I can let you know first part of the week. Promise."

She looked up at the telling gray clouds through the picture window of Susie's living room. A light wind was blowing the treetops. Brooke Lynn had one foot out the front door when an updraft brushed against her bare legs. When she grabbed the handlebars to lift her bike off the damp grass, the cool air touched the back of her neck.

"Wished I hadn't forgotten my jacket. Can you believe it's October already? Seems like we just started the school year," Brooke Lynn said.

She rubbed the goosebumps on her arms and shook off any ill feelings.

"See you later, alligator," Susie shouted.

Brooke Lynn veered right at the first corner. Her faint familiar reply resounded.

"…after a while, crocodile."

It was the same goodbye since 3rd grade, giving a positive nod that they were still besties.

Brooke Lynn looked forward to hanging out with Mike tomorrow. It had been way too long. She missed him more than she'd admit to Susie… or herself.

Chapter Four

NEW MIKE – NEW BIKE

When Brooke Lynn rolled up to Mike's house, he was shuffling his feet out front on the gravel path. His eye-roll would be next with an exhaustive sigh. And there it was – as though on cue. He could be a royal pain. Good thing they were pals!

"What took you so long? You only live five minutes way," Mike kidded her.

Her eyes squinted. "I had a last-minute call from Susie. You know us girly-girls!" Brooke Lynn couldn't resist giving a sarcastic answer.

Last summer, she began to see the changes in Mike. He had physically morphed into an older kid over the summer. Poof! Like magic! His face had grown longer, a couple of whiskers were popping out of his chin, and he'd sprouted up about six inches, towering over her. He seemed preoccupied with some new classmates. But the worst part – his texts had become less frequent.

Our *relationship **has** shifted… a consequence of growing up, maybe?*

"Let's go already. Where's your bike?" she asked, her words trailing off.

Mike came back out from around the corner of the house, grinning ear-to-ear.

"Hey, Brooke Lynn, check this out… surprise! My dad got me this rad new bike for my birthday – the one I wanted from Pete's Bike Shop. It was on my wish list. Remember?"

"Yeah, but why didn't you tell me earlier? It's, um… amazing," Brooke Lynn said.

They told each other everything, well, until lately. She felt hurt and disappointed.

"I wanted to surprise you," he added with enthusiasm. Mike was completely unaware of the slight Brooke Lynn felt.

"You certainly did that! It's cool, and I bet it's fast. Your birthday was last week though. Why haven't I seen you riding it to school?"

"It was on special order or I would've shown you sooner, BL. Geez! Pete didn't have a 5-speed in metallic blue when my dad and I went down there. It just came in yesterday. Freaking cool, huh?"

Brooke Lynn knew Mike's father had flown back to his overseas command post right after his birthday party. His job kept him away from his family for long stretches. Whenever Mr. Larkin was home Stateside, Mike spent all his free time with his dad. Usually quiet for a while after he left, she was happy to see Mike in a decent mood.

"Nice! I like it a lot, Mike. Let's break it in. Time to get dirty and explore," Brooke Lynn said.

With a bitter after-taste of 5-speed envy, she tried to keep up. She had admired the girl's version in Pete's Bike Shop just last week.

Maybe for my birthday?

"Race you. Hey, that's why I like bike riding with you; you're not one of those girly-girls," Mike joshed.

He often teased her about being a bit of a tomboy. In the past, she played along with him. But today, as soon as the words left his mouth, she felt offended. She knew she was being sensitive because of his lack of attention lately. They were a pair, almost inseparable… well, they *used* to be! Not wanting to ruin their time together, she squashed the resentment for now.

The duo valued being the "Two Keepers" of the neighborhood. They had been tagged affectionately as the *2-K Team* by some in the community. When things were a little odd, not what they appeared to be, Brooke Lynn and Mike did some casual snooping around to ease their neighbors' concerns.

This new housing project would be worth reporting about... plus, Brooke Lynn longed for a new case. It had been months since the last. They meandered through the streets and spotted Mr. Wilkens standing in his front yard.

"Hi there, Mr. Wilkens!" Mike waved.

Mike thought about last year's rewarding closed case. The elder man waved back.

"What are you working on today? Any new investigations popping up?" Mr. Wilkens bellowed across the lawn.

"The housing project, Oak Grove Homes – going to check it out, make sure they aren't closing town access to our bike and hiking trails."

They rounded the bend and the new site sprung up before them. The fresh exposed soil had been staked off into lots which seemed to go on forever. The parcels gradually climbed up the hillside reminding her of a dark chocolate layer cake. The tiered clearing stopped below the grey boulders near Granite Pass.

Unsure where the bike trail ran through the project below the pass, Brooke Lynn grew curious. They needed to investigate the grove entrance.

"Hey, Mike, let's stop for a minute," she called out.

Mike pulled over alongside of Brooke Lynn.

"I was thinking about, you know, Ladybug, your mouse. Won't take but a sec to pop over to his oak tree. That's the tree. Plus, I want to see if the entrance is still open to the trails."

She pointed east of the project.

"It's right over there – see it past that first mound?"

Leaving their bikes behind, they walked up the steep embankment. Brooke Lynn lightly tugged on his arm, pulling him towards the tree. She then dropped her clutch allowing him to walk the rest of the way alone.

Memories of helping him bury his beloved pet mouse flooded in. After his heart surgery, Mike got the mouse as a gift from his dad. When he named his new rodent *Ladybug*, Brooke Lynn thought it was a silly name. But she understood once he pointed to the black spots on the mouse's back.

Feeling a little sentimental, it reinforced that their friendship remained somewhat on track. Barely audible, she listened to his faint message from a distance.

"Miss you, little guy. I hope you're resting peacefully, Ladybug. You were the best pet. When Dad brought you home, you were good company. I will never forget you, Ladybug," Mike whispered.

Mike's head hung low until he started back, kicking a rock between his feet like a soccer ball. When he pivoted on his heels, he looked right at her.

Did my heart skip a beat? Get a grip, girl!

"Thanks, BL, for thinking about Ladybug. With all these trucks moving dirt around… he's okay, right?"

Turning away from his stare, something stirred deep inside her, almost a wild restlessness. She suddenly wanted to hold onto this feel-good moment.

Chapter Five

WHAT A SITE!

"Ladybug's resting spot should be okay. My mom said the planning group has the oak trees in the park on their agenda. She's been filling me in on the results of their meetings with the developer. The locals want to save the trees and have access to all the trails. Oh good, looks like the entrance is still open," Brooke Lynn said, relieved to see the development hadn't blocked the entrance. "This big ole oak tree isn't going anywhere for now."

"Race you," Mike said with a renewed energy.

At the mouth of the road, Mike yelled up into the clouds.

"I win!"

Instead of feeling green about Mike's new wheels, Brooke Lynn turned her attention to the white stucco buildings jutting up on the first hillside. In front were three half-built homes. Only one had a finished roof. She looked beyond the buildings with a newfound understanding of just how close the trails were to the construction site.

The low hum of a motor collided with Brooke Lynn's far away thoughts. By the time she spotted the fast-moving vehicle, it was too late. There was no way to warn Mike.

The blue pickup barreled down the hill at high speed. Brooke Lynn watched as all four tires left the ground. It jumped over the curb and landed about 20 feet away from them. Through the billowing brown cloud of dust, she strained to follow the vehicle through the main artery of the community. When the truck took a sharp turn to the right, it was gone from view.

"OMG… that was close. Geez, my mother warned me about coming over here. Plus, that guy wasn't even paying attention. It's almost 4:00. Think that's the last of the workers for today?" Mike choked, then coughed.

Brooke Lynn shook off the dust and shrugged at her pal, not quite sure if they should move forward. She wanted to at least have a fast look.

She noticed the *No Trespassing* sign posted on the unlocked entry gate. She ignored her instinct to turn around. Her eyes shifted away from the notice. After all, the gate *was* wide open.

"Let's just get a fast peek. We'll be in and out before we know it. Then we can say we saw the project before any of our friends," Brooke Lynn decided.

"But, BL, I don't think we're allowed on this road. There's a post," Mike said, pointing.

Brooke Lynn ignored his warning. She moved through the gate entrance ahead of Mike, over the rough path. They climbed up the steep short hill. Stopping at the top, they looked around for any activity.

Have all the construction crew left for the day?

They came upon the first nearly completed home. The neatly stacked lumber off to the side and a nearby sawdust pile triggered her to stop. The damp wood shavings prompted a brief memory of her grandfather's workshop. She was never allowed inside without permission.

"Wait, on second thought, this is probably as far as we should go. Kind of gives me the creeps with the machines around," Brooke Lynn said.

"Don't be chicken! We can always leave if it's dangerous. Brooke Lynn, really? Let's keep going. We *are* the *2-K Team*," Mike teased.

They inched ahead. Not wanting to disappoint her brave friend, Brooke Lynn followed, lagging a few feet behind. They hadn't hung out in a few weeks and she missed this part of their friendship.

"Next door isn't nearly as complete as this one," she observed. "Might be fun to check that one out too."

They leaned the bikes against the garage and walked through the muddy front yard of the first house.

"I wonder what the back area looks like," Brooke Lynn said.

They entered through the side gate into a small, fenced in back yard. She compared it to her huge, sprawling yard and felt much better. Flowering shrubs still in plastic containers sat ready for planting. From the rear side of the house, a single door – slightly ajar – lured them to come closer.

After a tick of silence, Mike put his finger up to his lips and blew.

"Shoosh, go slow."

With a deliberate foothold, he entered through the doorway into a small square room containing a utility sink centered next to the laundry hookups. Brooke Lynn was right behind him. At the far end of a long, smooth counter was another doorway leading into a dim hallway.

They stood there deciding which direction to go next. Except for Mike's shallow, steady breathing, all was still. Brooke Lynn hadn't noticed she was holding her breath. She released a much-needed exhale.

"Yup, everyone must have left for the day. Don't hear anyone." Mike hesitated. "BL, I just can't stop thinking about that speeding truck. What a jerk!"

Mike continued down the darkened hallway when a sharp, loud **BANG,** then a thunderous **boom,** rumbled through the empty rooms.

Brooke Lynn's jitters increased with each echo.

CHAPTER SIX

MYSTERIOUS SHOE

Brooke Lynn jumped back, clutching an imaginary jacket just as the tiny hairs rose on her arms.

Darn, why'd I forget my windbreaker?

They adjusted to the low light and found the nearest window. A lightning bolt shot across the thickening clouds outside. It appeared they had found the center of the home. Brooke Lynn twirled around the huge room with arms outstretched. Straight ahead was a grey-stoned fireplace with shelving on either side, she imagined her books stacked neatly on them. Her eyes moved up to the loose wiring dangling from the ceiling.

Boom! Brooke Lynn shivered at the rumble. She looked up half expecting the bolt to come through the roof. The sky illuminated again, sending intense flashes around the room. The flash made her see spots. It was like a rapid strobe light ricocheting off the walls. Her muffled cry escaped.

"Yikes... eek!"

I'm getting that creepy-crawly feeling... the one just before something's about to happen.

"Mike, I've got the creeps! I think we should leave."

Brooke Lynn wanted to be strong in front of her bestie. With both brows raised, her secret was out. As her mouth watered, she could taste her salty fear of thunderstorms.

Mike shook his head in disbelief. Locking into his stare, she envied his courage. He smirked, then moved on. Ever since Mike's recovery from his surgery, little seemed to bother him. She stayed close and in-step grateful he was by her side.

Mike's hand lightly touched the smooth wall while his gaze held onto the stone fireplace. When his arm came to rest on the rough edge of the mantel, she giggled. He stood tall like a king of his castle.

"I really like this place, BL. It feels, you know, kind of cozy even though this house is empty. I like the one room down the hall on the right. It has a view of the back yard. Be a nice bedroom. Which one would you pick, BL?"

"Not sure, let me go look again. It'd be cool to live in something so modern," she responded.

Brooke Lynn took another peek in each of the rooms, feeling slightly braver. When she got to the last one on the left, she nodded. This would be hers. She admired the sturdy built-in desk and bookcase. She started to turn away, when a lumpy object on the floor caught her eye. Something was just under the built-ins in the far corner. She rushed back to get her pal.

What is that dark clump?

"I liked the room on the left that looks out into the back yard," she said swiftly to Mike. "Then our rooms could be across from each other and have the same view! But you got to see something. Not quite sure what it is. Follow me."

He was on her heels at they entered the cold hallway on their way to the last room in the back. She felt his short breaths on her neck. The mini flashlight she had in her back pocket helped, but the beam was not quite bright enough. Its narrow rays shone on the dark cubby corner.

Another roll of thunder echoed off the ceiling and carried its baritone sound through each wall. It was followed by a loud **bah-bah-boom!**

"Here's... here's what I wanted to show you," Brooke Lynn stammered.

Peering over at the far corner, she aimed the low, slender beam onto the lump. She moved in closer.

Yup, in the very last room, far-away, tucked in the corner… something reddish-brown lay flat nestled down in the dark cubby of the built-in shelving. Brooke Lynn crouched down on all fours and inched up. She reached toward the unknown object, but her arms were too short; she couldn't quite reach all the way to the end of the cubby. Looking around the nearly empty room, she located a long screwdriver lying next to a bucket full of odd tools. Asking Mike to pull it out for her would be giving up!

Determined, she got down again in the prone position as Mike watched on. His breathing became rapid. Brooke Lynn stretched as far as she could, but still couldn't get the instrument to grab its edge. She took in a big, deep breath and with all the concentration she could muster, she made one final reach. The screwdriver snagged the item.

As she gingerly pulled it towards her, she realized it was a man's shoe – a well-worn brown dress shoe – with a red stain on it.

*Is this **blood**? And where's the mate to this shoe?*

The splotch was a good-sized splatter mark on top of the shoe. Brooke Lynn pulled it closer to them. She used the end of the screwdriver to pick the shoe up off the floor to get a closer look when – **smack**! It slipped off the end and dropped to the floor! A fine prickle ran down her back, causing the hairs on her neck to tingle. Her palms were clammy.

Calming herself, she slowed her breathing. Her hands trembled. She passed the screwdriver to Mike.

After a few wiggles, Mike was able to pick up the shoe with the tool.

"Let's go where there's more light," Mike proposed.

Retracing their steps through the hallway into the room with the large windows, the shoe hung loosely from the tip. It dangled, barely secured. She sucked in air, waiting for it to drop.

"Could be anyone's shoe, right? It's a man's left shoe," Mike said, examining the shoe in the better light. "It's nice, not cheap looking and it's made in Italy. It's an ancient style so probably from some old man. This may or may not be blood. I think we better put it back. Maybe someone is looking for their missing shoe. Or they hid it in the cubby on purpose if it's blood."

He hurried back to the bedroom and shoved the shoe back where Brooke Lynn had found it.

Brooke Lynn watched, then gasped. Mike turned around and saw where the beam of her torch was pointed.

Staring down at the concrete floor, they saw a stain.

Is this blood too?

It was a deep red color and was smeared around the edges as though it had been wiped up in haste. Brooke Lynn's heart raced. It seemed like the access to the bike trails was the least of their worries.

Chapter Seven

PUZZLING RED STAINS

The faint beam highlighted the large dark red splatter on the cement floor.

"Now this is a weird one, Mike."

They looked closer. In the middle of the room were darkish spray marks shooting across the floor. They were about three feet or so across. It was a significant spill of sorts and had been roughly cleaned up. Of interest to Brooke Lynn, the faint reddish mark on the shoe was a match.

Yikes! It sure does look like blood.

"Will you look at that! It's got a red-brown tint too just like the shoe. If it's blood, then someone may have gotten hurt. I'll have to put my bigger flashlight in my bike pouch so we can get a better look around next time," Mike said.

"Next time?" Brooke Lynn felt excitement. "Let's head out now. It's getting dark."

Brooke Lynn glanced over at her fellow sleuth and remembered Susie's request to check the site out with them at the weekend. Why did it feel like an ongoing struggle between her besties? She brushed the whirling frustrations aside.

Her focus returned to the unanswered questions. Between the stain on the cement floor and the shoe, well, something was off here!

Whose shoe is it and what happened to the person wearing it?

"Maybe someone cut themselves and removed the shoe to clean it later," Brooke Lynn mused. "I'll check the newspaper in case anyone has gone missing recently or there is an accident reported at this project." She needed to do some investigative research.

The rain pounded on the roof with a steady force. A relentless wind begged the question - was it safer to stay inside until the storm let up? The house was only partially completed after all. They stood in the middle of the room deciding their next move. **Bah-BOOM!**

Their rapid looks at one another said one thing.... **RUN!**

They galloped out of the house, Brooke Lynn remembering to leave the door just as they had found it, slightly opened. They didn't want the construction crew to know anyone had been snooping around.

With pants and shoes covered in dark muck, each step felt heavier. Dragging their bikes away from the soggy ground, they waded through the huge mud puddles. Brooke Lynn could just make out the slickened street ahead by the glow of the tall streetlamps. The high wind and sheets of rain made it hard to focus.

What time is it and why are the lights **on** *already?*

"BL, are you okay?" Mike braced himself with a secure grip. "It must be late. I'm taking the short-cut through Mrs. Hardiman's side yard. See you tomorrow."

"Yeah... tomorrow."

Brooke Lynn rounded the next street, and saw a vehicle headed in her direction. Oh boy! As it drew closer, she recognized it as the same blue truck they had seen leaving the construction road earlier. Whoever was driving wasn't paying any attention to the speed limit!

Her body tensed up as she counted the seconds until it passed. She prayed he'd miss her.

Brooke Lynn jerked the handlebars toward the sidewalk. Her knuckles had turned white from her tight grip. She locked her elbows to brace for impact as the truck sped by - just missing her, but not the huge puddle. As though in slow-motion... **S-p-l-a-s-h!** She was drenched.

The driver hadn't even given her a side-glance when he passed. But the tell-tale dent on the rear bumper and a partial plate number, LS19, might prove helpful to the *2-K Team*.

She focused on the wet road ahead, steering clear of any large potholes. Wiping out now wasn't an option! Wet and chilled, but in one piece, she arrived home and entered through the garage side door. The wind slammed it shut.

So much for sneaking in undetected.

"Is that you, Brooke Lynn?"

Chapter Eight

NEW RULES

"Yeah, Mom. I'll be down in a minute. We got a little wet out there. It's really coming down," Brooke Lynn answered.

She tossed her soggy shoes and dirty socks to the side. Mud tracks in the house wouldn't bode well right now.

"Don't forget to set the table," her mother hollered.

Brooke Lynn ran up the stairs barefoot, two at a time and tripped on the next to the last step. It sent her face-first into the well-worn landing. Luckily, she had left her muddy shoes by the side door or there would have been trouble.

She quickly changed into a pair of comfy leggings and her favorite worn T-shirt. Time was an issue. She needed to get the table set before her mother asked again. Taking two steps at a time down the stairs, she missed the last two and landed with a familiar **thud**.

Oh no, Whoops!

"Brooke Lynn, remember what I said about running and jumping down the stairs?" her mother cried.

"Whatever! I'm trying to be careful about running down the steps. Geez, Mom, I can't do anything right lately."

As she walked into the kitchen, Brooke Lynn couldn't hold back with her sassy reply. She was tired from the ride but also sick of her mother's constant requests.

She's so negative about everything I do!

"Just try to slow down," her mother pleaded.

Brooke Lynn bit back another snotty answer. She felt like she was failing on all fronts. Between school, her friends, and chores, it was a balancing act. Up until recently, Brooke Lynn and her mom had gotten along for the most part. She wasn't sure how to fix their tense relationship.

"Brookie, can we talk?" her mom asked. "I know you and Mike like to explore after school, but your chores come first and that means getting home in plenty of time to clean up and then set the table. Flying in the door at the last minute in a frenzy, well, that's got to stop, that's all I'm asking. Just slow down. Are you wearing the watch I gave you? It might help."

"I know, I get it. I just feel like you're always yelling at me. I *am* trying." Brooke Lynn frowned.

She didn't know how to make things okay with her mom.

Now, where did I put that watch?

She drifted to her last birthday when she got to pick out the watch she'd been wanting for a while. It was the first time her mother had let her personally choose her own gift.

"What about these over here? You can pick any style you'd like; sporty or dressy, it's up to you. I got my first watch when I was about your age from my mother. It really helped me to be more punctual. I want it to be something special that you like, and that you'll use," her mother had said.

Stocked with different wrist bands, Brooke Lynn finally set her eyes on one that had a stopwatch feature. It was still stylish and would come in handy when racing Mike.

With 56 other reminders, she'd have to add this to her to-do list - #57- **put on watch** each morning!

Brooke Lynn fiddled with the silverware. When she came around the table, she hesitated. She didn't want to start anything with her brother, but she needed to finish the place settings. Arnie was scrolling on his cellphone and didn't look up.

"Can you move your elbows so I can finish setting the table, please?" She waited for his usual snide remark.

Arnie leaned back his chair tilting it up on two legs before answering his sister.

"Alrighty then! Hey, Babbling Brooke, Mom's mad at you. I heard her saying something about you're always late."

Brooke Lynn gave him a snarl but opted to ignore the comment.

"Mom, anything else you need on the table?"

"Nope. Table looks good. Thanks. And, young man, what did I say about snapping at your sister? She asked you nicely, Arnold. Now, take your elbows off the table. I'm sure your dad had a rough day at work - they've been short-handed and he's having to put in long hours. So, can you both please try to get along?"

Arnie clunked his chair back down and huffed.

"Okay, I'll do it for you, Mom. She's such an easy target but I'll try."

Her mother frowned but dropped the conversation. Brooke Lynn watched her mom's face soften as she pulled the casserole from the oven. She inhaled the cheesy, aromatic warmth it offered while it bubbled up.

"Brooke Lynn, would you please get your dad?"

When everyone was finally seated, Brooke Lynn looked across at her brother. Geez, she thought her brother ate like it was his last meal, but she wasn't going to start anything tonight. The sounds of chomping in between the pinging of forks hitting their plates must have annoyed her dad. The scowl on his face was obvious.

"Gosh, slow down everyone! How about we go around the table and talk about what we've been up to for a change?" her dad asked.

Brooke Lynn snickered quietly. She could visualize them as zombies bumping into one another, bouncing off the walls. No one responded to her dad's question. He shook his head.

"In fact, I think your mother has some new rules she'd like to discuss. It's the perfect time for some changes."

Oh boy, here it comes...

Chapter Nine

BIG BROTHER

Her father rarely became agitated, but when he did, she knew to pay attention. Brooke Lynn sat quietly, selfishly hoping the new rules didn't apply to her. The stare from her mom told a different story.

"What? I'm listening," Brooke Lynn reassured her.

"Like your dad mentioned, I'd like to implement some changes around here as a family. From now on, no phones at the table, household chores need to be carried out without continually being asked, no running through the house, chairs have four legs for a reason - please leave all four on the floor, let's try being on time – punctual, yeah? I know we all make to-do lists but as the old adage says, *Actions speak louder than words*. Well, it still carries weight."

"What the heck, Mom. No phones until when? After the last bite or away from the table completely?" Brooke Lynn asked.

"No phones at the dining table *at all*. Come on, guys, you can at least put in the effort. I'm serious," her mother said.

They all shook their heads slowly, somewhat agreeing to the rules.

"Good, it starts tonight. Turn off your phones please. Arnie, that includes you… you first, tell us about your day."

They took turns sharing without interruption and begrudgingly – no phones. Brooke Lynn looked over at her brother and smirked. He rolled his eyes in disbelief. For that split moment, Brooke Lynn felt they were on the same side.

After taking her last bite, Brooke Lynn jumped up from the table. Rather than check her phone, she started clearing the table.

No sooner had she washed the first dish when her brother picked up the dish towel, wiping as she cleaned. With the last of the plates put away, she finally broke the silence.

"Hey, Arnie, so Mike and I went over to the new homes to check them out. And you know the Oak Grove Park where we used to climb that big old tree?"

Her brother nodded, so she continued.

"Well, I wanted to make sure nobody from the construction site was chopping any of those trees down. You know the hiking and bike trails that run along-side of the project, heading up toward Granite Pass? We're hoping the developer doesn't cut off the entrance to the trails from the rest of the town. So far, there's no changes. The whole project is cool though. You should pop over for a look. It's massive."

"Hey, is that swing I fixed like six years ago still there? I haven't been over to that park area or the hiking trails in a while," Arnie asked.

"The swing's still there and it works minus a few splinters. I think I got a sliver the last time I tried it. Have you seen Mike lately? You wouldn't recognize him. He looks like one of your football players. I guess he worked out all summer playing soccer or something."

"No, I haven't seen him in a long time. He was always so sick looking and scrawny. I did hear he was playing soccer though from one of my teammates who knows him. I'll have to stop by to watch him work out on the soccer field. Little Mikey," Arnie mused.

"I heard you have a new girlfriend. What's she like?"

"Who told you, nosy? Mom, I'm sure," her brother said irritated.

"No, I couldn't care less... just thought I'd ask. Forget it," Brooke Lynn quickly added.

"Okay, wait, sorry. Um, her name is Belinda, she's a cheerleader, let's see... she's funny. Oh, she's a real brainiac too, like you. We're just getting to know each other, nothing too serious but I think she's pretty cool. You'd like her."

"I like this, Arnie. Can we try to be more like this, you know, where we aren't picking on each other? It feels kind of nice," Brooke Lynn suggested. "Maybe I could meet Belinda one day?"

"Does it really bother you when I call you Babbling Brooke?" Arnie dodged the question. "I'm just kidding around. Mom told me I shouldn't tease you so much. I can see how it could be irritating. Yeah, I mean, uh, I guess we can both try."

Arnie twisted the wet dishtowel, gave it a snap just missing the side of her hip, then tossed it on the counter. He flashed a mischievous smile.

Maybe, older brothers aren't so bad after all.

She knew she could treat him better too… it worked both ways.

"I'm going to go do my homework, Mom. See you in the morning," Brooke Lynn said, yawning.

"Thanks for helping. It was nice to see you two getting along. See you in the morning, Brookie," her mother said.

Brooke Lynn didn't like it when her mother called her "Brookie". Ick! She had reminded her mom lots of times. Brookie sounded babyish to her. She let it slide and slowly climbed the stairs to the sanctuary of her room.

She picked up the science textbook and remembered she had a pop quiz tomorrow! Re-reading the two last chapters they had reviewed in class on Friday, she scanned her notes. She stared at the same page, but it all looked like jumbled words.

Where has the weekend gone?

She texted Mike asking if he got the same surprise science quiz as her class.

"YUP ☺ SUP?" he texted back.

"ASK ME ?S," she texted.

Back and forth they texted each other about the insects they were studying, until her final text.

"☺ W2G TA CUITM."

Just before closing her eyes, she remembered that she hadn't asked Mike if he was okay with Susie coming along to the site. Had it truly slipped her mind? She'd ask tomorrow.

Chapter Ten

POP QUIZ NIGHTMARE

Brooke Lynn struggled to fall asleep and when she did, it was short-lived. Unable to remember the exact details of the nightmare, she lay awake staring up at the shadows on the ceiling. Wiping the back of her clammy neck with her nightgown, the feeling was evident.

Doom... what am I dreading?

At some point, she managed to doze off. When her eyelids popped open, there was light coming through the sheer curtain. She blinked the dryness away. With a thread of memory about the scary dream, she squinted in shock at her bedside clock. It was already 6:30. All she wanted to do was roll back over.

...something about failing a test.

Thankfully, she told herself it was only a dream. Surely, she had studied enough.

Missing her younger years when her mother used to sit on the edge of her bed after a bad dream, she shrugged it off as childish. She dragged herself out of the warmth of the down comforter. Turning to make the bed, she groaned.

Being responsible, huh? New routine indeed.

Without dilly-dallying, Brooke Lynn got ready for school. Loosely braiding a side ponytail, she gave a lasting glance in the mirror. She approved. Descending the stairs in her stocking feet, she sniffed a familiar aroma – fresh, brewed coffee.

A little miffed from last night's new house rules, she entered the kitchen softly. She blurted a greeting louder than normal to her unsuspecting parent.

"Good morning, Mom!"

"Ah-oh, good morning. I didn't hear you come in. You startled me. How'd you sleep?" her mother replied.

"Not good. I had a bad dream. I couldn't get my brain to slow down."

"You finished your studying over the weekend, right?" her mother asked.

Brooke Lynn rolled her eyes, then stretched her arms overhead and flexed.

Gosh, she can be such a pain.

"Y-e-s, Mom. I wish you didn't always think the worst. Like I didn't study or something," Brooke Lynn sighed.

She saw the snarled look on her mother's face. Brooke Lynn didn't want to be mean to her. But irritation was all she felt. She loosened the muscles in her stiff neck, rolling her head side-to-side. As she fought back a tear, a pull of regret subdued her angst.

"I just couldn't get to sleep… that's all."

"Oh, I hate it when that happens to me." Her mother understood. "Hey, I was just reading in the paper about the new project. Says here the town is still concerned about the Oak Grove Park and picnic area, along with the oak trees by the property line. Plus, there's an issue about the trail entrance staying open to the locals. I sure do hope that gets resolved soon with the developer. Be a shame if there's no access."

Her mother paused as she looked at her daughter's seeming disinterest. Brooke Lynn was aware of the town's challenges but her thoughts were on her immediate problem… the pop science quiz. Shifting from one foot to the other, she tried to stand still as she listened.

"Speaking of the project, I have been thinking some more about you and Mike exploring over there. I saw the *No Trespassing* signs posted around the fencing of the property when I drove by yesterday. Do me a favor and talk to the construction manager before you go onto the property. I believe you need to get permission first. Otherwise, your father and I don't want you over there. It's too dangerous," her mother said.

Hurry up already!

"And, Brooke Lynn, when you talk to the foreman or manager, mention the speeding trucks zipping through our neighborhood too. The traffic is still a problem," her mother finished.

"I know, right? When we went by there yesterday, no one was around except one crazy speeding blue truck. Luckily, I got part of his license plate number. So, *if* the manager is in, I'll tell him about the truck but, if he's not, I'll leave him a note under the door of the trailer. I'm not sure if we saw a notice, but the gate was wide open. I'll look next time we go over there."

Brooke Lynn felt a bit sneaky about the sign. It was clearly marked. Her comment was in part true though - the gate was unlocked.

"Okay, but be careful and check first," her mother warned.

"I just think I'm just a little restless about the pop quiz," Brooke Lynn assured her mother.

"Okay, Brookie. Your dad's already left for work and your brother had early training, so whenever you want to go, I can give you a ride."

"Thanks, but I'll take my bike. And, Mom, can you try to stop calling me Brookie. Remember? I don't like it anymore… sounds like a baby name."

"Well, that's because I've been calling you that since you were a baby," her mother mused.

Brooke Lynn could tell her mother was a little put off by this latest request, but she stood firm.

"All right, fine. I'll quit saying it then, and good luck on your test today. See you later."

Brooke Lynn rinsed her dishes off before flying out the door. She pedaled as fast as she could - bookbag comfortably on her back

- cycling the two miles to school. She should have time to review her chapters once more. A tiny stab of guilt seeped in.

Did I study enough for the test?

No sooner had she sat down on one of the courtyard benches when Mike saddled up.

"Hey, BL. What are you doing?"

"Just a quick look before school." Brooke Lynn moved up, making room on the bench for Mike. "I had a bad dream last night about the science test. I think I've got it though."

"You're the smartest girl I know… you'll be fine. Plus, we tested each other last night. 'Member? Well, see you," Mike said, not taking a seat and instead walking away.

Brooke Lynn watched, as he walked off toward a group of friends, wondering where she fit in. Were they still best friends?

Chapter Eleven

BALANCING ACT

With remnants of her dream hanging around like an embedded splinter, Brooke Lynn concentrated on the pages in front of her. When the first bell rang, she followed a handful of stragglers inside.

Before Brooke Lynn knew it, the tests were being passed out. She scanned the quiz sheet. Immediately spotting several questions that were unfamiliar, her ears started to burn. She tried to swallow the panic away. The noise from the timer sitting on the front desk grew louder with each passing tick.

When her pen slipped out of her hand, she wiped her sweaty palms on her pants. She picked up the smooth pen and wrote the first answer, then raised her hand.

"Yes, Brooke Lynn?" Miss Hart asked.

"The chapters were six and seven, right?" Brooke Lynn questioned.

"Yes, why do you ask?" Miss Hart replied with arched brows.

"Oh nothing, thanks," Brooke Lynn said, hurrying to finish in time.

The stress of juggling friendships and school life had her torn. Hanging out with Susie and then goofing around with Mike at the development had preoccupied her time. Brooke Lynn hated to admit to herself that she had messed up! She was unsure of her answers. She rolled her eyes in her sockets, closing each lid.

I could just spit nails I'm so mad at myself.

Next was English which she loved. Miss Hart was lecturing about the next term paper, *Being Open Minded,* and the importance of the assignment toward their final grade for the semester. It was due next Monday. As the teacher wrapped up the last subject, she asked everyone to see her on the way out.

"Class, overall, I was disappointed in the science test scores. I've added comments to each of your tests. Please take note of my comments," Miss Hart told them.

Brooke Lynn waited her turn. Inching up in the line, she finally reached Miss Hart.

"Wait over there, Brooke Lynn. I want to talk with you."

What is this about?

Doom was all she sensed, just like when she woke from her dream. After the last student filed out, Miss Hart called to Brooke Lynn.

"I noticed you didn't get all the answers correct. Based on your student record from previous grades, it seems unusual for you. You missed seven of the 20 questions, Brooke Lynn. Don't get me wrong, a C+ is still an average, okay grade, but A's have been the norm for you. I know you can do much better. Did you study for the test? Is something going on I should know about?" Miss Hart asked.

"C+! Really? Oh no, are you sure? Did you double check my answers? Miss Hart, I promise I did study but… well, I guess, not enough…"

Brooke Lynn tried to explain, but it sounded weak even to her. Miss Hart stood with arms crossed and both eyebrows raised. Brooke Lynn sighed.

"No excuse, Miss Hart. I have been distracted with personal things. I will do better. Thanks."

She was bummed. It was the first time she had gotten anything less than a B+. She walked to her locker in a self-absorbed trance. Hadn't her parents said that her grades could affect her future? One bad grade… come on, really? But her mother's words replayed in her head.

Make sure chores and studying come first before hanging out with your friends. Ugh!

Thinking whether she needed to tell her parents or let it slide, she trembled at the thought.

Once outside of the building, she hurried to her bike. The light breeze of the unusual, warm day touched her bare arms. When the embarrassing thoughts disappeared, she was still mad about her quiz. She held her head up toward the sun, shutting her eyes. It had been a rough, emotional day. Life wasn't getting any easier for this 7th grader!

Mike yelled out, startling her. She blinked her eyes open.

"Hey, Brooke Lynn, I can't go explore the construction place today. Bummer, huh? My mother texted a reminder - I have a dentist appointment about braces. Yuck-o! I don't want braces, but she wants me to get my bite checked out. Could be worse, I guess."

Her friend was baling out on her. What else! She did feel for Mike though, especially if he were to get teased. She could already imagine what the kids might say if he had braces.

"Yeah, bummer! Braces, I feel for you, buddy. Well, I'm going to ride over there anyway. I want to talk to the manager about the speeding truck and see what's happening over there. I'll fill you in, okay? Oh, I almost forgot, Susie wants to come with us to the construction site, like maybe this weekend. What do you think about her tagging along?" Brooke Lynn asked.

Mike paused for a sec. "Hmm, not sure… I guess I always thought of her as too… I don't know… prissy. We can get grimy. It's called the *2-K Team*, remember? No room for a 3rd wheel."

"Well, she said the entire town is invited to the grand opening party at the site. It's in a couple of weeks. She just got a flyer with all the info. And there's some big secret about *who* the new homeowners will be. Susie is dreaming about a celebrity moving in. Geez, I doubt it. Anyway, it sounds like a cool event with a live band and tons of food. Everyone's probably going," she said. "I don't think Susie wants to come with us to get involved in any kind of case or getting dirty."

Brooke Lynn was glad in a selfish way that Mike wasn't too keen about Susie joining them, but then she remembered Susie's hopeful face. She felt caught in the middle, maybe they could make it a quick visit. That would satisfy both friends... she hoped.

"It does sound like a big deal," Mike hesitated. "The party and everything."

"Yeah, I'm sure that's why she's curious. Can you at least think about it? What about this Saturday afternoon?" Brooke Lynn said confidently.

"I guess so... yeah, it'll be all right. I'm going to Susie's right after my dentist appointment today. She's tutoring me on the upcoming English term paper. I'm stuck and she offered to help me today in class. Mr. Clemens said these papers count a lot toward our grade. I'll let her know Saturday afternoon will be good for her to come with us."

As Brooke Lynn rode away, something tickled her neck. She rolled her shoulders around as though adjusting her shirt. No, it wasn't an itch. It was the thought of Susie and Mike spending time together.

Tutoring, huh? He had always come to Brooke Lynn if he had trouble with any schoolwork.

CHAPTER TWELVE
SOLE VISIT

Feeling left out, Brooke Lynn pedaled home feverishly. Growing up was so hard! Wanting to be a good friend to Susie *and* Mike, well, it felt like a tug-of-war at times.

See, our friendship is changing!

Brooke Lynn rechecked her attitude and called Mike right away. It went straight to his voicemail instead.

"Hey, thought of this… you'll have braces off before we're in high school. See you, pal," she chirped into the phone recording.

Something still bugged her; Mike and Susie spending time together - alone. She felt sorry for herself.

Why am I so eager to be around Mike?

Brooke Lynn grabbed the leash off the hallway hook. Her canine cutie Samantha Sue would keep her company. She needed to make a delivery.

"Come on, happy Sam. Let's go on a walk, girl," she resolved.

As they walked at a steady stride, Brooke Lynn wondered how many new families would be moving into the Oak Grove Homes. Then, she chuckled at the thought of them picking out their rooms yesterday. Such silliness let her know their friendship was intact.

She had grown up in the same two-story house since she was a little girl. Although some of the homes looked a tad worn and weathered, she loved her unique, tree-lined street. Its brilliant oranges, purples and red leaves during autumn were magnificent! The colorful umbrella of old foliage was quaint and cozy.

When Samantha Sue and Brooke Lynn arrived at the site, a disappointment stirred in her. The entry gate was closed and locked. The posted notice glared back at Brooke Lynn to keep out.

Oh no... now what?

She spotted the trailer marked "Construction Office" across the road, but it was on the other side of the gate. Unsure of how brave she truly felt, she stammered out loud to Sam in hope of finding some courage.

"Let's, er-um, let's go check out the trailer in case anyone's around, okay, buddy? We just need permission."

Seeing a small opening in the fencing about 50 feet down on the left, she tugged at Sam's leash and led the way. They made the climb, keeping the trailer in sight.

Brooke Lynn peered through the dusty window of the big metal trailer. It was too dark to see inside. She knocked on the rickety aluminum door and waited. After a long minute, she reached into her back pocket and pulled out her crumpled note. Flattening it, she shoved it under the door through the narrow gap. She hoped the manager would see it.

If anyone questioned why she had trespassed onto the site, Brooke Lynn had a cover story - she was certain the information she was providing couldn't be delayed any longer. The speeder needed to be stopped, right?

She walked her pup around the corner of the same house she and Mike had explored. The side door was ever-so-slightly open again.

Her uncertainty was on full display when her hand twitched reaching for the doorknob. Something prompted her to look over her shoulder at the new build next door. Was there movement inside?

She looked across until her eyes rested on a shadow dancing across the windows. A gust moved one of the sprawling branches of a pear tree against the rough exterior of the home. Its scraping noise gave Brooke Lynn a spook. In unison with the wind, a cast of shapes floated onto the glass panes, then disappeared. She exhaled.

On second thought, she wasn't feeling very brave. She'd wait for her crime-busting pal for the next round of investigating.

"Okay, Samantha Sue, that's enough for today."

Never happier to be walking up their driveway, she tilted her face up toward the warm lights showering the facade of her family home. She imagined the heat seeping out toward her. Yes, she loved her childhood home. Noticing her dad's car in the driveway already, she felt safe.

Feeling her wrist, she had forgotten her watch again. So much for working on being time-savvy!

Oops, am I late?

When Brooke Lynn stepped inside, Samantha Sue looked up with her sweet puppy eyes. Panting from her trek, her pet was hungry. She felt the tug at her heart for not having spent much time with her lately.

"Come on, girl. Let's get you some fresh water and food."

"Almost time for dinner. You're late," her brother teased.

She brushed his snicker off. Brooke Lynn headed into the kitchen and looked at the table. It was set for dinner, minus the hot items.

"Hey there. Thanks, Mom, for setting the table for me. I was running a bit late. I brought Sam along and she moves a lot slower than me. No excuse, I know… I will make it up by cleaning up after," Brooke Lynn offered.

"Oh, hi, Brooke, and no you weren't late but you can thank your brother for helping you out this evening," her mother replied.

"I owe you, Arnie," she called out.

"No worries. I'll think of something for you," Arnie said with a grin.

Brooke Lynn bit her lip just as her stomach growled. Her mom's homemade spaghetti sauce smelled extra delicious this evening. She hadn't eaten much all day.

Brooke Lynn put the rest of the dinner items on the table. As she looked up at her mom swiping a wisp of hair away from her brow, an appreciation stirred inside. For some unknown reason, she had a yearning to learn about her mom's sauce recipe. It prompted the sensation of comfort each time the aroma floated up her nostrils.

"It smells so yummy, Mom. Can you please tell me what smells so special? What's the secret?" Brooke Lynn asked.

"Ah well, it's a dash of nutmeg. But the extra kicker is *when* you add the secret ingredient. Next time I make it, why don't you help and I'll show you how I put it all together?" her mother offered.

Brooke Lynn watched through the oven window as the cheese topping bubbled up on the garlic bread. Right before the edges turned dark brown, she grabbed the mitt off the counter and pulled out the slices. She was starving. Trying to be more of a help, she set the bread in the basket, then on the table.

"Mom, I had kind of a rough day at school," Brooke Lynn whined.

"You did, yeah? How'd you do on the science test?" her mother asked.

Brooke Lynn fought back a tear. Then she blurted it out... expecting the worst from her mother.

Chapter Thirteen
OPEN-MINDED

"Well, not the greatest. I got a C+. I missed seven answers. I'm so mad at myself about it!"

Before her mother could get a word in, Brooke Lynn jumped in again.

"I know, I know, Mom, before you say anything… I know I need to balance my time better between my chores, school, and spending time with my friends. I feel so bad already. But I know what to do to get back on track."

Brooke Lynn knew she was babbling but she was sick about her low grade. Her mother was about to say something but stopped and just listened. By all appearances, Brooke Lynn was doing a decent job of beating herself up. Her mom reached for her daughter's hand, then changed her mind mid-way, grabbing the iced tea pitcher instead.

After listening to Arnie's story about his new girlfriend, Brooke Lynn noticed his face light up when he talked about Belinda. They were getting friendlier… even more than he was letting on she suspected. She wondered what it would be like to feel that way about someone, then shrugged the thought from her mind quickly.

"You guys should see what's going on at the site," Brooke Lynn said, trying to steer the conversation away from relationships. "Three homes are almost done. We've been careful too. The entrance to the trails and park area is still open for now. I looked around for the manager, Mom, but he wasn't there so I put the note under his door. I'm curious to know what he says about it, I hope he calls me about the speeding truck."

She stopped talking, reminding herself not to mention what she had found; the stained shoe and bloody cement floor had the young sleuth wondering what happened over there. It was a mystery which had turned into an unexpected investigation. But she wasn't ready to reveal that part of her story... yet.

There was something else she wanted to talk about though in relationship to the development.

"Oh, one last thing... did we get a flyer about the Oak Grove Homes' grand opening party, Mom? Susie said they got one, but I haven't seen ours. Lots of talk about it according to Susie. I'd like to know what it says out of curiosity."

"Yes, we've got a flyer – it's tacked up on the fridge. I guess it's going to be a huge event per Annie Larkin as she's part of the planning group. I think it's in about two weeks. The rumor mill around town has everyone guessing about who'll be buying the first home. Not sure why it's a secret unless it's some celebrity. Anyway, I'm looking forward to it. And your father and I love a good live band too," her mom said.

One of Brooke Lynn's favorite desserts, pumpkin bread drizzled with a light velvety vanilla glaze, was a perfect surprise ending to the meal. She wished they could have dessert every night.

"Thanks, Mom, for the yummy dinner. I'm so full." Brooke Lynn patted her belly.

Arnie was half-listening while fiddling with the last bites on his plate.

"May I be excused? I have to make a call and I have some homework I've got to get done tonight."

Brooke Lynn thought her brother looked distracted. Maybe something to do with football or his new girlfriend. Probably why he was testy at times.

What? No snide comments?

"Of course, son. Thanks for helping with the table-setting. See you in the morning. And Brooke Lynn, you can help me clean up since Arnie helped with the table," her mom stated.

"That's what I promised," she said.

Brooke Lynn started clearing the table. Her dad chimed in after being quiet through most of supper.

"Hey, Brooke Lynn, your mother and I really want to emphasize that you should be careful over there. Speeding truck aside, there's a lot of heavy equipment. But I do like that you are interested in the town's overall well-being. It's nice to see you involved in things other than schoolwork," her father said.

"Thanks Dad, I appreciate it. I will let you and Mom know if we find anything weird over there. We are being careful."

Should I tell them about the bloody shoe?

She'd wait until she and Mike investigated further **before** telling her folks. With a bit of doubt, she hoped Mike would know what to do next.

"Hey, Brooke Lynn, I know you like checking out peculiar things in the neighborhood. Just let me know if you need my help. I'm terrific at catching boogey men." Her brother walked away laughing.

She could hear him making snorting sounds all the way up to his room. Brooke Lynn wondered if this was her brother's awkward way of looking out for her.

Yeah, right!

"Let's skip the handwashing tonight. There's plenty to load the dishwasher up," her mother said.

With her brother and her dad out of the kitchen, Brooke Lynn sensed now was a good time to bring up bra shopping. Plus, she needed to confirm it with Susie soon.

"Mom, I, um-er, well, I have something to talk to you about. I was talking with Susie on Sunday, and she agreed with me, well, it's time for me to get a bra. She said a sports bra might work to start. I agree and think it's time. Can you take us shopping?" Brooke Lynn asked, handing her one last plate.

She diverted her eyes to the dirt smudge on the kitchen floor. Brooke Lynn could feel her mother looking at her. Unsure what to do next, she wiped the counter one more time.

"Well, can you stand up straight? Okay… yeah. I was just waiting for you to come to me when you were ready. And I think it's time, Brookie. Oops, sorry, Brooke. But a sports bra? I mean, I guess, well, to start. Try on several options first though. And you want Susie to come with us, right? I know you enjoy her company."

"Yeah, I was hoping it would be okay. Saturday morning?" Brooke Lynn asked.

"Okay, this Saturday morning about 10:00 after our chores. That works," her mom said.

"Perfect, I'll let her know. And, Mom, thanks. It's not easy for me to talk about these things." Brooke Lynn squirmed.

"I understand, honey. It gets easier to discuss personal, intimate things in due time," her mother reassured her.

"Thanks again. Sam, race you up the steps! Night, Mom."

Brooke Lynn let out a sigh as she tackled the nagging term paper. She wrote the title of the assignment across the top of the page: *Being Open-Minded*. The thought of speaking in front of her class made her skin prickle.

This paper *had* to be her best! Her stomach lurched just thinking about the science quiz grade. Ugh! She tucked the notepad back in her bookbag for the night. The idea of being open-minded about the new development was her topic for the essay. The investigation might add some findings for the paper.

But first, she opened her iPad, clicked on a new folder titling it, *The Case of the Hidden Shoe*. This investigation was officially opened. Now all they needed was more clues.

Chapter Fourteen

WHO IS MR. CLEMENS?

When Brooke Lynn awoke and saw the time – 7:30 – she yelped. *What the heck! Oh no!*

She rushed, madly throwing on an outfit of a black and white striped shirt with a black and white polka dot pair of cropped slacks, then slid into her black flats. It was a bit crazy and wild compared to her usual easy-going look. She had second thoughts.

Flashing back to Susie's smart wardrobe, she had another go at it in the mirror. She liked her own style too and smiled. It felt, well, kind of FUN to wear something unexpected. She tucked her fly-away messy hair inside a red felt beret… that was her carefree mood that morning.

Brooke Lynn grabbed a breakfast bar out of the pantry and started toward the door.

"I'm running late, Mom. Got to dash. See you after school."

Her mother's head poked up from the newspaper.

"Bye then, have a good day. Oh, did you sleep better last night?"

"Yes, Mom. Busy day again. Bye."

Glancing sideways at her mom, Brooke Lynn kind of missed their pre-school chats. But lately, she was feeling the stronghold of wanting her independence. She kept walking out the door in the direction of her bike.

When did life get so confusing, almost a battle?

Her life needed some adjusting to even out the struggles she felt. She passed by a group gathered by the bike stand. Not recognizing any of the kids, she locked her wheels and noticed Mike's bike already parked. For some curious reason, Brooke Lynn felt more confident today. Maybe it was the thought of a new case. She stepped into the school corridor feeling an inch taller.

The investigation had her baffled. She couldn't stop thinking about the red stain on the shoe, plus the odd stain in the middle of the floor. If only she were certain that it was blood. It made her dizzy. She needed to focus on her schoolwork. Good thing she was an avid note-taker!

Returning her attention to the teacher for like the ninth time, the bell startled her as though it was a fire drill. Racing down the stairwell toward the doors, she almost ran head-on into Susie. Instead, she side-swiped Mike. He twirled around on his heels, hopping on one leg, then regained his balance. Mike looked at his turbulent friend, then did a double take.

"Whoa, slow down, BL. You almost knocked Susie down too. What's the rush?"

What was different about BL? New hat maybe? He couldn't figure out what he was noticing. What a goofball friend.

"Oh, sorry guys, did you get my text?" Brooke Lynn swiftly asked.

"I sure did. Saturday morning and afternoon both look good. I need to be home by noon though. My mom wants me to help her for two hours babysitting my little brother. But she said I could go back out at three. She's interested too about what's going on over there. Maybe we'll spot the movie star she saw? Truth is she likes the gossip! See you," Susie replied.

"Wait a sec, like as in celebrity? Who did she see? What have you heard?" Brooke Lynn inquired, grabbing Susie's arm before she rushed away.

"My mom thought she saw an actor on her way to work. She couldn't remember his name or what movies he was in, but his face looked familiar. Anyway, she said he was coming out of the clinic yesterday morning with a bandaged hand. She couldn't get a clear view because he was surrounded by people right before he got into a black limousine. Maybe he's buying a new home over there? Cool thought if it's true, huh?"

"Huh, it is... see you later," Brooke Lynn wondered.

"I've been looking for you. Where'd you go at lunch break?" Mike asked as Susie hurried away to go home.

"I skipped going to the cafeteria and decided to eat outside in the courtyard for a change. Such a sunny warm day," Brooke Lynn said, smiling.

"Okay well, I got something *big*. You are not going to believe this. My favorite teacher, no wait, best teacher *ever*, Mr. Clemens, was wearing an identical pair of shoes as the one we found at the job site. His shoes looked the same. Geez! And get this, the left shoe had a faint darkish smudge on the top, you know, where the leather was a different shade? Could have been a red stain and then been wiped off. Maybe that was *his* shoe at the house!" Mike said.

Brooke Lynn's ears perked up. She released a light gasp while her pal continued.

"Weird, huh? Anyway, he asked to speak to me after class. It's like he has this sixth sense or something. Anyway, I could not believe my eyes when I looked down at his shoes, BL. If I'm mistaken, it's an awfully close match. But when would he have gone to the house to get the shoe? That's got me stuck!" Mike stated.

She stopped his rant by interrupting him. He was too worked up.

"Maybe he is buying a new home there? Or he was visiting a friend at the site? Something happened like a fight or disagreement or... I don't know."

Brooke Lynn started wondering about Mr. Clemens. He was a suspicious character with those strange sideburns and wanting to speak to Mike after class as if he knew they had been at the site. Who was he truly? Baddie by night, good teacher by day... she needed to find out. Was the actor's injury connected to the blood-stained project? Mike's trusted teacher might be involved. Her sense for mystery was tickling her to look deeper.

"Wait," Mike interrupted her thoughts, "there's more!"

Chapter Fifteen
GET A CLUE

Mike picked up where he left off. He was spinning into a wild story.

"I told him I liked his shoes. Then I asked him if they were Italian by chance. And, get this, he said YES! He bought them when he was in Italy a few years ago and asked me why! I was so nervous, but I wiggled out of it by saying I was curious, that's all. So, they *are* Italian just like the shoe at the house."

Brooke Lynn tried to follow his train of thought but switched gears instead.

"Whoa! You're jumping the gun, Sherlock. The solo shoe may still be at the house which makes your theory prove diddly squat… think it through, Mike."

"Well, at the end of class, he announced he didn't want to hear any more chatter about the site or guessing about the new homeowners. He told us we were talking too much about it in class and should be paying closer attention to our subjects. Weird, huh? It must have been his shoe at the house that we saw, but…" Mike finally stopped.

Brooke Lynn swayed back and forth giving the appearance of a heavy thinker, but she knew it was uncertainty. Brooke Lynn needed a new angle. Where was her gut intuition when she needed it?

"What would he be doing over there, Mike? How come we didn't run into him? Okay – okay, I got it! Maybe Mr. Clemens went back to retrieve his shoe, saw our bikes, and waited until we left? That's why he asked to speak to you today. He's keeping you close in case you get suspicious about him. Or he feels guilty maybe over harming the new homeowner… or worse. You know that actor Susie's mom thinks she saw was injured somewhere. Did it happen at the site? So many possibilities."

Brooke Lynn continued, "Either way, he could be on to us snooping around the house, so we should be careful. If he's guilty of some wrongdoing, then we need to find out fast. Favorite teacher or not, let's try to follow him after school. Mike, I think we have our first clue since finding the shoe and opening the case."

Mike smiled at her cleverness. But he didn't like that their suspicious person of interest was Mr. Clemens. This could be exciting… or dangerous!

"Mr. C. is my favorite teacher of all time. I hope he's not up to something bad. For my sake, I need to know." Mike frowned.

At 3:05, teaming up as planned, they walked their bikes to the faculty parking lot, and hid behind a rusty parked van. About 10 minutes later, they watched Mr. Clemens come out of the building and get into his car. They pedaled as fast as they could to keep up, but only got as far as the next block before he drove out of sight.

"Now what? Keep cycling to the job site in case he ends up there? We need to know if the stained shoe is still at the house," Mike said.

"I agree we need to know," Brooke Lynn said, but a nagging feeling was making her uncomfortable. Her mother's words about taking her homework more seriously floated round her head. She was torn. "But the more I think about it, well, it sounds like a far-fetched chance that he was heading there right now. Plus, I've got a lot of homework to do. How about tomorrow? I can get caught up on my studies tonight. Okay?"

"Okay then. But tomorrow we need to get inside that house to check on the shoe. If it's in the house, then Mr. C. is innocent, right?"

Mike was trying to convince himself more than Brooke Lynn.

Once home, Brooke Lynn grabbed a pile of old newspapers stacked in a basket by the sofa, she knew she should have started her homework right away, but she couldn't shake the mystery from her mind. She flipped to the Local News section of the paper to see if there were any reports of an injury at the building site. Nothing. Turning to the Entertainment page there was no report of any injured or missing actors. But perhaps it hadn't been reported… why would Mr. Clemens report it if he were guilty of harming someone? She tossed them back in the recycle basket. Dead end. Time to face homework.

Early Thursday morning, the blue light blinked steadily on her phone. Brooke Lynn was annoyed that it might make her late for school. She stopped getting dressed to listen. It was a message from someone she didn't know but the company name gave her hope.

"Um, Brooke Lynn, this is Joe, the construction manager at the Oak Grove Homes project. Thank you for leaving the note at my trailer. I've taken care of the issue. We appreciate the detailed info you provided. Stop by the trailer when you get a chance so I can personally thank you."

As she stood in front of her locker listening to the recorded message again, she couldn't wait to tell her pal. Just then she shrieked. Mike had snuck up from behind.

"Eek, stop it! You know I don't like being tickled! Hey, I've got some good news. I received a call from the construction manager at Oak Grove saying he got my note and took care of the issue. I hope that means he figured out the speeder," Brooke Lynn said.

"That's great news. Do you have time to swing by the site before going home today? Remember, we want to check if the shoe is still there. I just need to know," Mike asked.

"Sure thing, but let's make it brief. My mother isn't real keen on me being over there. She saw the *No Trespassing* signs. If the manager is in his trailer, we should ask if it's okay to look around. I could even introduce myself as the person who left the note," Brooke Lynn said.

"Yeah sure. I just need one quick peek. Shouldn't take long," Mike assured her.

When school was over, they hurried over to the site. Several crew trucks had passed them on the way; not one of them was speeding. They even waved to her as they passed. Nice change. And the gate was open – a bonus for sure. Mike circled his bike around Brooke Lynn. He was anxious and ready.

Brooke Lynn wondered why sometimes the gate was open and other times it was locked. When they rode up the incline, she had her answer. *He* must have unlocked the gate. Mr. Clemens' funky yellow car was parked in the first driveway. No mistaking his dull mustard four-door clunker.

Chapter Sixteen

MIKE LARKIN SHARES

Seeing Mr. Clemens' car made Brooke Lynn forget about any attempt in getting permission from the site manager.

They could hear male voices coming from inside the house towards the back bedrooms. Stepping cautiously in through one of the side entries, they hid under the nearest kitchen counter. Speaking with hushed tones as though intentional, the children overheard Mr. Clemens' voice.

"You keep getting this wrong, Joe. I'm worried I'm going to get in trouble. Heads will roll if anything else gets messed up! We're running out of time. What part of this don't you understand? Get it straightened out soon, and get this place cleaned up too. See what you can do about this stain right away before anyone sees it. I'll be bringing my personal client by soon for another walk-through. And let me know if you hear any more gossip about that celebrity. Let's keep this incident between us," Mr. Clemens said.

"No worries, Mr. Clemens. I've got some chemicals that will get rid of this stain. They'll never know it was there when I'm done with it," the Joe guy replied.

Mike whispered, "I can't believe it. Whoever this Joe fella is, well, he's helping Mr. Clemens. I just can't figure out what they're up to, can you? Something's got him bothered though. They don't want any evidence of the blood or whatever left around. And who's this personal client of Mr. Clemens? Maybe the new homeowner? He mentioned the gossip about the celebrity but I don't know what that means."

Brooke Lynn thought there was something sinister about the conversation. Their low tones seemed intentional, almost like a coverup of sorts by Mr. Clemens.

The two separate sets of footsteps walked firmly down the main hallway. One of the side entry doors opened and shut moments later. The door handle was being jiggled. Mike heard a CLICK.

The conversation faded as the men moved further away from the house. Only when the car door slammed closed did they dare poke their heads up.

"I think the coast is clear to come out. Watch your head. Let's wait a few more minutes before leaving," Mike said to his crime-buster partner. "What's Mr. C. doing here and who is Joe? Some construction guy, perhaps?"

"Mike, I forgot to tell you who the call was from this morning. It was from Joe, the construction manager. Must be the same person. I'm confused though about Mr. Clemens. What would a teacher be doing at a housing project? He said something about bringing his client here. What if the personal client *is* the first homeowner like you said? Like he's doing some real estate deal or something. And just maybe it's the actor with the bandaged hand that Susie's mom saw in town? That would explain the blood."

Mike smirked at his friend's theory. He shook his head not wanting to believe it. His pal had an imagination. She'd never understand his mixed feelings about Mr. Clemens.

From the beginning of the school year, Mr. Clemens had paid special attention to Mike and his schoolwork. He was like a male role model and exactly what Mike needed in his dad's absence. He just couldn't imagine Mr. C. harming anyone.

"Come on, I need to know once and for all if that was Mr. C.'s shoe. It's bugging me," Mike answered.

Brooke Lynn and Mike ventured back out into the hallway. In a flash, bright headlights lit up the wall nearly blinding them. They dropped to the floor and huddled low until they heard tires crunching over the graveled drive. The vehicle finally drove away.

With not much daylight left, they adjusted to the dimness of the house.

"Let's see if the shoe is still in the cubby. I want to take another look at the floor stain too."

Mike remembered he'd forgotten his flashlight as they walked the gloomy hallway. Brooke Lynn bent down, spying the untouched shoe. The only thing peculiar was the stain had been wiped clean with barely any visible sign of the dark, reddish marks.

"Well, I guess someone owns an almost identical pair of shoes as Mr. Clemens since this can't be his - you said he was wearing his pair. So, who is missing their shoe? I know – Cinderella!" Brooke Lynn giggled, then snorted. "Lame I know, Mike, but for now, *The Case of the Hidden Shoe* is still ongoing until we figure out who is missing a shoe and if anyone got hurt or worse. It has to be someone Mr. Clemens knows or is involved with."

Although Mike wanted his teacher to be innocent, they both had a distrust about his extra-curricular activities. There was a sneakiness about Mr. Clemens' secretive meeting.

"Well, we can take Mr. C. off the list as far as that being *his* shoe. But it doesn't clear him of any wrongdoing either. It does make me question where this investigation is going," Mike said, somewhat relieved.

"I think we're done for the day. Let's boogey out of here," Brooke Lynn suggested.

"How the stains got there and *why* it was hidden... this mystery is unsolved. I mean, why hide it in the dark corner?" Mike asked, realizing he had more questions than answers.

Brooke Lynn headed for the door, walking ahead of Mike by a few paces. She heard Mike's footsteps halt.

"What's up?" she asked.

Mike was standing in the doorway of the great room. Brooke Lynn joined him and watched as he went into the room. Her friend sat down on the fireplace ledge and gazed out the front picture window. His jaw muscles bulged as he clenched his teeth. She watched him, concerned.

"Are you okay?"

"Can you stay a little longer? I just need to talk," Mike asked slowly.

Patting the area next to him, she took a seat. His head was bent down like he spotted something on his high-tops.

"It's been weighing on me and I just need to say it before I burst!"

"Of course, spit it out." Brooke Lynn was a bit unsettled about what her friend was going to say, she waited.

Her mind started reeling. He might share something she wasn't ready to hear. He and Susie *had* been spending more time together.

What if he has feelings for Susie? Ugh!

Mike sucked in air like he was ready to take a deep plunge underwater. Brooke Lynn tensed up as he exhaled.

"I HATE IT WHEN MY DAD LEAVES!"

His words were so loud she almost covered her ears. Brooke Lynn stayed silent… glad it was about his dad.

"I don't talk about it much because it hurts. But, when my dad was here for my birthday, it really made me miss him. He'll be home again next week, but it's not the same. He'll have to leave again. Each trip home he tells me he'll be working Stateside someday soon. But when?! I really could use his advice, you know, on guy stuff. It's so frustrating! I just needed to say it out loud."

Mike swallowed hard revealing his exhaustion. His naturally tanned cheeks couldn't hide the wet streaks coming from his glossy eyes. He wiped the evidence with the back of his sleeve as he drew in another deep gulp stifling a hiccup.

"I can only imagine, buddy, what it's like. He will be home for good one day. Trust him. He wouldn't say it unless it were true." Brooke Lynn started to reach for his hand but rubbed his arm instead. She waited for him to regain his composure.

Thankful for her dad more than ever, she realized that her two closest friends didn't have their fathers around. What an emotional load. In that shared moment, it confirmed they were still close.

"I'm glad you told me how your dad's absence has been affecting you. I had no idea. Come on, Mike, are you ready to leave?" Brooke Lynn asked, nudging his shoulder, and catching the boyish look on his twisted face.

They made their way in silence down the hallway and towards the door.

Brooke Lynn grabbed the brass handle, but it was locked! She turned to her stunned buddy. Mike thought back to the jiggling and CLICK he'd heard after the rushing footsteps. He looked back at her with worry.

"We're locked in," he said with urgency.

Chapter Seventeen

GIVE AND TAKE

"Hey, let me think… there's got to be a lock inside somewhere…" Mike mumbled.

Mike located the deadbolt above the door handle. He turned the toggle once until he heard it click. Then promptly twisted the door handle, but nothing happened. He gave the deadbolt toggle one more hard turn in the opposite direction. The additional click sounded promising. With another attempt at the doorknob, it freely swung open. An initial look of relief on Mike's face indicated they were in the clear… until Brooke Lynn saw his alarmed expression return.

"What now?" Brooke Lynn said.

"Uh oh, we have a problem. How are we going to lock it back up so no one knows we've been here tonight?"

"We can go out through the garage and crawl under the garage door before it closes. I hope," Brooke Lynn suggested.

Relocking the deadbolt, they exited out into the garage. When Mike located the door opener on the garage wall, he pushed it once and the rolling door rose. Right before he pushed it again, he looked over at Brooke Lynn.

"Okay, we can do this. It'll be close though. When I say *go*, run fast," Mike said.

With less than two feet of clearance, they dropped and rolled under the rapidly descending door. When they heard the garage door snuggly close behind them, they bounced straight up and brushed themselves off.

"Whew!" came out of their mouths.

Walking their bikes down the hill, the entry gate was also closed and locked. Brooke Lynn looked down the fence line. She pointed to the known gap in the fence to the right. They pushed their bikes out first and then wiggled through the narrow opening.

"Man, that was close. Too close," Mike muttered.

After heading their separate ways, Brooke Lynn's phone rang. She was surprised to see it was Mike calling already.

"Hey! You've only just left me!" she said with a smile.

"I just thought, what if the missing shoe owner is someone we know?" Mike's voice was full of excitement. "Let's keep our eyes peeled for anyone else besides Mr. C. wearing similar shoes. Oh, a-n-d guess what?"

Brooke Lynn heard Mike's excitement by the cracked pitch in his voice. She snickered.

"What – what?" she replied.

"I've got a message from my dad. He's flying home late this evening instead of next week. I'm so relieved, BL. So, I know we promised Susie to tag along this Saturday but I want to spend time with him. Just depends how long he's in town this time. You know? I'll keep you posted."

"Didn't he just leave only a few days ago? Oh well, no worries, your dad's visit takes priority. I can take Susie over there by myself but I'd rather have you there with us," she answered.

Oh geez, that sounds pathetic!

"I mean... just in case we discover something else. But I understand. Later then," Brooke Lynn said.

Brooke Lynn hung up just as she arrived home and was letting herself in the door. Her mom was waiting for her.

"There you are, Brooke Lynn! We were wondering when you'd decide to come home. Were you and Mike tied up over at the new project again?" her mother asked, then sighed loudly.

Brooke Lynn heard her monster mom's disapproving tone. After her last grade, plus the challenges with Mike and Susie, she was not in the mood for a lecture. Short of gnawing her toes off, she'd rather do anything but listen to her mother complain.

A guilty feeling set in deep, she probably should have been studying. Balancing her life between home, her friends and school felt like a festering skin rash. Her shoulders caved.

"This new case you and Mike are working on, well, be sure it doesn't interfere with your schoolwork. I just want to make sure your studies are getting done. And have you gotten permission to be over at the site like I asked?" her mother said.

When Brooke Lynn didn't respond, her mother switched the subject surprisingly.

"Your dad wants to treat us to dinner at The Wheelhouse in town for their Swedish Meatball Night. You need to be ready in about 15 minutes. Sound good?"

"I guess. I am starving. Um…" Brooke Lynn sighed. "Mom, you sounded annoyed about our investigation. It isn't silly or a waste of time, you know? We're just trying to help by being the watchdogs of the neighborhood. Plus, I think it's good research for my English paper."

Brooke Lynn was still a bit ticked off at her mother for harping about her new investigation. Preferring to hang out with Mike over studying was what she wanted to do. Once they got more answers, she'd come back around on her priorities. It was best to keep the details of their case quiet from now on.

Chapter Eighteen

SNEAKING OUT

To make peace with her mom, Brooke Lynn let up on her tone.

"Sorry for letting time slip away, Mom. The construction manager thanked me for the tip on the speeder and said he's taken care of the issue. Oh, and he left me a message to come by to talk to him any time. We *are* helping and we have been careful."

"Okay, you know, Brooke Lynn, I've been trying to give you your space to figure things out on your own. It just wears on me when you go against what I've asked," her mother said.

She walked over, standing face-to-face with her daughter, then reached out but stopped short. Unsure whether to hug her, she picked up Brooke Lynn's hands and held them in hers.

"It's a give and take thing, honey."

Brooke Lynn let go of her hand, avoiding eye contact. Why was she feeling so bad? She didn't want to squabble.

Before stepping outside, she grabbed her sweater off the hallway hook. Grateful for remembering it, the sharp night air nipped at her flushed cheeks.

When they entered The Wheelhouse, the hostess escorted them to a red vinyl-covered booth. The sweet smell of cinnamon had Brooke Lynn thinking about dessert already. Holding back a snicker, the waiter approached the table wearing lederhosen. Brooke Lynn tried her best not to gawk. While he filled the water glasses, he recited the specials of the evening.

"And… who's ready to order?" offered the server.

As the first meal arrived, Brooke Lynn's phone started ringing. She scrambled to turn it off, then gave an apologetic look.

"Sorry, guys, I thought I had – er, I promise it's off now. I know the rule."

Boy, if looks could kill!

Brooke Lynn savored the last bite of apple pie, and then pulled out her phone. Before her mother eyed her movement, she returned it to her back pocket with a self-conscious shove. The blue blinking light would have to wait.

New rules, huh!

In the back seat heading home, Arnie started tapping out a text. Guessing it was safe, Brooke Lynn reached for her phone and read her long-awaited message.

"URGENT… MEET @ 8 2nite @ site."

It was from Mike with no specific details about *why* tonight! She had never snuck out before. How was she going to pull this off? Sighing, she didn't want to let her crime-busting pal down. It was risky. Brooke Lynn read it for a third time until the car rolled into the driveway.

What is so important?

Brooke Lynn sat down hard on the sofa. Checking her watch, it was now 7:20. She pulled a loose strand of hair and twirled it between her fingers; an unconscious nervous habit when concentrating.

Okay, it's decision time!

She texted Mike back she'd be there. The thought of getting in trouble had her torn. Brooke Lynn sat waiting until she mustered up the courage to make up the story.

"Mom, I need to work on some homework. Another big day tomorrow. So, good night," Brooke Lynn stated.

Am I rebelling against them… or myself?

"Okay then, I'll see you in the morning, honey. Say good night to your father too," her mom responded.

"Good night, Dad. And thanks again for taking us out to dinner." A soft punch of guilt hit her when her dad looked up at her. The "good girl" that he often called her was 20 minutes away from being bad.

She fought the reluctance to be honest with one justified thought - she would tell them eventually... well, only *if* she needed their help.

Upstairs, Brooke Lynn rumpled her bed. Looking out into the hallway, she noticed her brother's door was closed. He was probably studying. She crept down the stairs, stood on the bottom step, and listened. The hallway grandfather clock chimed 8:00. Her heart pounded to the steady chatter of her parents. It was time to make her escape.

Brooke Lynn, like a ninja, rolled her bike to the end of the drive. Luckily, she had a small headlight mounted to the front handlebars. She hoped her parents stayed up late watching their show so she could sneak back in without incident.

Conflicted by excitement and nerves, she felt giddy. She cycled with a fierceness up to the construction road. She was a few minutes late. Mike's silhouette was outlined against the white-washed stonewall. A jolt of tension ran across her chest.

So, this is what naughty feels like!

"Over here. Keep your voice down. Two voices are coming from inside the first house. Probably Mr. C. and his client," Mike whispered.

"So why exactly did you need to meet tonight?" Brooke Lynn demanded.

"Shush! When my mom and I went out for pizza, I saw a light on in the first house. Two shadows were moving around inside. I wanted to check it out. The man with the missing shoe might be inside and he might be the celebrity client too. Whatever. We need to find out."

They set their bikes against the wall observing Mr. Clemens' faded yellow car in the driveway. Walking around the corner, they looked at the door previously left open. This time it was shut. Mike turned the handle carefully, but it didn't budge.

Darn!

"Let's look in through the big windows along the back. Maybe we'll be able to see them or at least hear a bit better?" Mike suggested.

"I'm not sure about this, Mike," Brooke Lynn said, her voice shaking slightly.

A lamp illuminated the room softly, but they could only tell that it was two men. They couldn't see their faces. At last, they recognized Mr. Clemens' low voice. The other mysterious person stood about half a foot taller than Mr. Clemens. He was talking more hushed than the teacher.

Mike's look of alarm startled Brooke Lynn. As his eyes grew wider, she waited for him to explain. Something had him disturbed.

Chapter Nineteen

CLOSE CALL OR NOT

"BL, one guy kind of sounds like my dad, but that's impossible, right? He's not flying in until later this evening. Nah, he's just been on my mind. I guess I'm tired. What would he be doing with Mr. C. anyway? What a weirdo I am," Mike admitted.

They tossed that wild thought away as they strained to hear. Who was this stranger? Why were they here so late?

"I don't know about this, Mike. I can't get a solid look at him with his back to us, and the closed window is muffling their conversation. Wait, he kind of sounds like Mr. Colby. Maybe he's the secret homebuyer? At any rate, this is a bad idea," Brooke Lynn said.

"Mr. Colby, as in our 6th Grade teacher? He did wear those dorky shoes. Yeah, that's interesting," Mike replied.

Trying to get a better angle, Mike moved a few steps to the left when – **BANG!**

Brooke Lynn couldn't believe their luck; Mike had bumped into a trash can. As the contents of the tipped can scattered into the yard, the lid took off rolling. When the lid came to a full stop, they only had seconds to hide.

Ducking down on all fours, they slithered under the window, crawling on their hands and knees in the rough dirt. Edging around the corner of the house, they hid behind the newly planted bushes.

"Good thing they've put these in," Mike whispered.

Through the leaves of the young shrubs, they looked over at the damage. Litter sat in clumps on the ground. That's when the side door swung open.

His breath was almost visible from the misty air. Mr. Clemens stood silent in the cool night. His head pivoted around while scanning the yard. Walking to the corner of the house, Mr. Clemens stopped.

"Look over there. Now I see what made the noise," Mr. Clemens stated.

He was pointing in their direction with the stranger standing behind him just out of view. A prickly feeling scooted across Brooke Lynn's skin. She stifled a sneeze.

"The trash can was knocked over. Probably just a stray cat. It's time to go anyway. I've got an early morning. I need to stop by here before my class starts. If any questions arise over the next few days, just let me know. We'll be cramming in a lot this week," Mr. Clemens said.

"Sounds good," the stranger answered.

Still unable to get a clear shot of the man, Mike thought if he could just poke his head out… but then stopped short. He wasn't feeling very brave. They waited.

When they finally heard the back door being locked, the two sets of footsteps walked toward the front of the house. Soon the teacher's car drove away.

"That seemed like forever. We better hurry home. I was hoping we could get inside to check on the shoe tonight and get a look at the other guy, but it doesn't look good. I heard them lock the house back up. If my mother realizes I've been out this late, she will ground me forever," Mike said.

"I don't want to get grounded either. It's almost 9:00. I might just make it before anyone notices I'm not in bed. I wish we could have figured out who the other guy was with Mr. Clemens. Maybe next time," Brooke Lynn agreed.

Mr. Clemens must have locked the entry gate on his way off the property as it was visibly secured. The children managed to squeeze through the sliver of an opening through the fence as before. Just as they made it through, they spotted a uniformed security guard standing at the gate checking on the lock. Was he new? They ducked into the shadows. He didn't look like a friendly sort. He glanced up and down the fence line. Finally, he took off on foot in the opposite direction. They'd have to be more careful in the future.

It was 9:08 when Brooke Lynn walked her bike to the side yard at home. Carefully, she opened the back door and listened. Hearing her mom and dad laughing at the TV, she lightly treaded up the stairs letting out a *phew* under her breath at the top of the landing.

After tossing her clothes on the corner chair, she felt heaviness in her arms from the tension. She glanced one last time at her phone - no text from Mike. She wished he'd have let her know he had made it home and to his room undetected. She texted him anyway.

"SAFE ☺ CU L." She pressed send.

When had she become so pooped? Slipping into her comfy nightie, she slid happily beneath the covers.

Chapter Twenty
A HUNCH

Brooke Lynn was awakened by the rustling sounds of a household already aroused and bustling. Lying there she remembered what she and Mike had done the night before, and threw the covers back over her head, wanting to stay there all day.

But instead, Brooke Lynn shot up from her bed, got her bearings, and hastily dressed. She plugged her phone into the charger and checked to see if Mike had texted back… nothing. Strange. She brushed out her hair, then rushed two at a time down the stairs.

Her mother called to her from the kitchen. In her preoccupation with "the guilts" from last evening, she couldn't imagine what her mother wanted.

"Young lady, come here please! What did I say about running down the stairs, Brooke Lynn Gale?"

Brooke Lynn was relieved her mom was talking about the stairs and not about last night's escapade.

"Sorry about that, Mom," she muttered softly.

Jeepers.

"I appreciate the apology, Brookie, I mean, Brooke Lynn. Here's some breakfast before you take off. I'm meeting Mike's mom for lunch and then my garden club, so I won't be here when you get home from school. Oh and, we're eating out at The Larkins' tonight, so I need you to be ready by 6:00 sharp. They have some sort of special announcement and have invited our family to dinner. I know it's kind of last minute but it sounded important."

Brooke Lynn wondered what the big occasion was all about. This was turning out to be quite a strange week. She turned back to her waffles and freshly sliced strawberries piled in front of her and slathered on some butter. With one long pour, she layered the golden waffles with the gooey syrup.

She contemplated what lay ahead in her day, taking the first bite. Had Mike gotten caught coming home last night? Brooke Lynn wanted to get back upstairs to check her phone. She thought the worst!

She didn't see Mike at school or hear from him all day. She tried to keep busy doing homework rather than dwell on his demise. When she heard her mother come home, she went downstairs to catch her before she got too busy.

"My homework is nearly all done, Mom. Do you need me to help you with anything? What did you and Mike's mom talk about at lunch today?" Brooke Lynn asked, hoping to get a hint at whether Mike was in trouble about sneaking out.

"Oh, the usual," her mother seemed distant. "I think there'll be lots to discuss tonight."

Uncomfortable and wanting to change the conversation, Brooke Lynn switched the subject.

"Do you have time to answer some questions about the development? I have a few areas I need to understand to finish my essay paper. You might be able to fill in what's been agreed upon with the developer. Lots of kids are wondering about the trails too, plus other things."

"Nice to hear you've been studying. Help me with these groceries first, okay? Then I'll try to answer some questions. Oh, have you seen your brother?" her mother asked.

"I think he's in his room probably doing schoolwork too."

As her mother unpacked, Brooke Lynn pulled her pad out from her school bag.

"Okay, overall, what are the top concerns about the project? How are they being addressed by the town's planning group with the developer?" Brooke Lynn asked.

"Traffic, saving the oak grove trees, the picnic area and, um, access to the hiking trails. Most items have been resolved. Annie Larkin has been keeping me in the loop. She said at lunch today that the main challenge now is with future buildouts. Smythe Development still needs to agree to more open space in the next phase. The township in return will agree to the additional homes. The next meeting should reveal the final voting results," her mother replied.

After answering several more questions, Brooke Lynn felt more enlightened about the project. She hoped to get the final vote results before her speech. Not even a minute after completing her interview, her dad came through the door lugging his briefcase. His shoulders sagged as he placed the heavy case on the nearest wooden chair.

"Hi, honey, hello, Brooke Lynn, getting hungry, ladies? According to Ernie, er, Mr. Larkin, his wife is whipping up a feast tonight. Her roasted chicken is to die for, I must say. And remember, we need to leave the house by 6:00."

"Yup, six, sharp!" Brooke Lynn and her mother chimed together.

Brooke Lynn got the clue and went upstairs to get cleaned up. She heard her brother's footsteps tromping down the hallway. She instinctively tensed up. When he simply waved, she relaxed her shoulders. Maybe he was trying, she hoped.

At six sharp, Brooke Lynn hurried out to the running car. Her dog followed her out, ready for her doggie playdate with Mike's pup.

"I get shotgun! Hey, Dad, Mike asked if Samantha Sue could come along too. He thought Sassy would like the company. Won't be a bother. Up – up, in the back, Sam!"

She slid into the front bucket seat as her father leaned in toward her. He spoke just above a whisper. Brooke Lynn moved closer, resting her elbow on the center console.

"I'll let you in on a little hunch about this special dinner tonight. Okay? It's just my gut feeling though," her dad said.

She stared at him as he spoke, not wanting to miss a word. Her dad was the most-handsomest man she knew. His smile softened his tired eyes, especially when he looked at her mother.

Mushy love, oh brother!

"My hunch is Mr. Larkin is going to announce he's returning Stateside with a new command post so he can be closer to home. Maybe like on the West Coast. I mentioned to him last summer I thought Mike needed him around more. And, selfishly, I want my old buddy back here too," he said.

"I hope it's true, Dad."

Brooke Lynn caught a familiar whiff of his after-shave cologne. Her dad confiding in her was huge. The revelation of his secret wish made her feel a little bit more grown up.

"And not a word out of me," she said crossing her heart.

Chapter Twenty-One

THE ANNOUNCEMENT

Arriving at The Larkins', Brooke Lynn retrieved her furry friend from the SUV rear hatch. Arnie's athletic legs sprinted to the door first, giving him honors to ring the doorbell. She read the message on the doormat out loud, more for herself than the others.

"WELCOME * Good Friends * The Spice of Life!"

"Hi everyone, come on in. Hope you're hungry!" Mike welcomed them.

"My mom made a feast. Mr. Gale and Arnie, my father is in the living room if you want to go there first. Mom said dinner will be ready in about 15. Hey, Brooke Lynn, come with me for a sec," Mike said, giving Sam a quick pet. "Hi, little Samantha Sue. Our Sassy is excited to see you. It's been a while, little fella. So, I've got something important to tell you, BL. It can't wait."

Through the patio slider, Mike led the way. Brooke Lynn and Sam hurried behind.

"Hey, was your dad home already? Did you get in any trouble? My parents didn't notice, but I was worried about you. Why didn't you return my text?" Brooke Lynn asked.

"Nope, no trouble, my mom was on the phone when I got home talking with my dad. He didn't get home until I was asleep. Sorry I didn't text you. Guess I forgot. Ah, look at the pups play… just like old buddies. Okay, okay, I have to tell you before I burst! I think my dad's announcement tonight might be he's retiring from his command post overseas."

He waited for her reaction. She didn't want to slip up and reveal her dad's secret hunch. Instead, she listened.

"He hinted about being home permanently on his last trip. I've given this some thought. And now him coming home so soon, it feels like he's been working on something. Oh man, I want this so bad." Mike stared over at the pups, a wishful look in his eyes.

Brooke Lynn had butterflies in her stomach, Mike's innocent, crooked smile was sweet in a boyish way. She tried to smash down the flitting and confusing sensations.

What is this about?

Brooke Lynn motioned as though she was zipping her lips.

"I hope your hunch is right."

She stepped within reach and gave him a loose hug. A bit self-aware of her display of affection towards him, she waited for him to say something – anything! There was an awkward pause.

Really?

Mike let go of his inhibitions by gesturing with a full fist pump.

"Yeah, I'm stoked! It's just a feeling, I hope I'm right!"

Mike finished his animation with a knuckle bump to his buddy. Brooke Lynn collected herself, smiling at his over-the-top joy.

They went inside to join the others. Brooke Lynn felt at-ease with her pal once again.

Annie Larkin, Mike's mother, was chatting with Sally Gale, Brooke Lynn's mother, in the kitchen. The laughter from the two mothers drew the rest into the room.

"Sally, thanks for the lovely flowers from your garden. You really do have a green thumb! Speaking of green, can you believe the size of those new energy-efficient homes?" Annie exclaimed. "Imagine the kitchens? I heard they have two ovens! But, girlfriend, we've made great memories here in this little kitchen, who needs two ovens anyway?"

"Ah, what are you two chatting about?" Mike's father, Ernie, asked. "You must be talking about the new homes going in. Just hope they take care of the traffic concerns through our neighborhood. I don't like the idea of all the congestion it might cause to our area."

Mike's mom wiped her hands on her apron and brushed a curl off her cheek.

"You know what they say about idle hands... since everyone's here, grab a bowl or platter from the counter. Then, let's get this dinner party rolling," Annie stated to the group.

In no time, the well-decorated dining table looked complete with not an inch of space left on the tabletop. Once seated, Mr. Larkin started passing around the food platters and bowls family-style. Right before the first bites were taken, Mr. Larkin gave his stemware a couple of taps with his fork.

"Everyone, I am excited to say, no – extremely delighted to say – after 25 years, I have finally retired from the military."

Gasps and happy whoops met Brooke Lynn's ears. She was so glad that her father and Mike's hunches had been correct. She looked at Mr. Larkin and noticed how his smile sparkled when he looked over at his wife. She set her eyes on her buddy. He was a mini version of his dad.

Why haven't I noticed this before?

"I am officially a civilian, and after a few days off, I'll be looking for some work. Hey, Mick, keep your eyes open for me. So, cheers to being retired from a long military career and finding a new job. And a big thanks to my wife and son for being so patient. You are my world! Okay, let's dig in," Ernie said.

"Now we can get a hoops game in, Ernie! Hey, Mike, you haven't seen anything until you see me beat your dad at b-ball." Mick Gale, Brooke Lynn's father, laughed.

She looked across at Mike. He wasn't eating much, just grinning while he observed everyone. She spotted his eyes welling up. Just before the first tear fell down his cheek, she kicked him hard under the table.

"Hey, happy for you, pal! Time for the dogs to come in?"

She was looking out for him. Mike would have been embarrassed if he had started sobbing at the table. He pulled his napkin up and gave his face a quick swipe.

"Going to let the pups inside. Back in a sec," Mike excused himself.

"Okay, is everyone going to the Oak Grove open house party? Free food and ice cream from Hammond's, yeah?" Brooke Lynn asked. "Still wonder who is moving in over there. My guess is it's someone from out-of-town like a big celebrity. Any guesses?"

"Maybe you're right, Brooke Lynn. Nothing passes through *Sweet Tarts Bakery* without me hearing any news about our residents. Must be an out-of-towner," Annie Larkin said. "Some famous actor was spotted coming out of the clinic by Rita Reynolds. But without a name, heck, it's only a rumor. Still… I have been on the lookout. And so far, I like what I see when I drive by the homes."

"Too much gossip, ladies, about the new homeowners," Mike's dad said. "Crazy stuff. And you kids should stay away from that busy construction zone. It's dangerous to be riding near it. Like I said earlier, Annie, I still have too many concerns. I'm just not sold on the development yet. But I'll save a dance for you, Mrs. Larkin." Mike's dad winked at his wife.

Brooke Lynn gulped at Mr. Larkin's warning. They still had unfinished business at the site. She had questions about sneaky Mr. Clemens. Afraid she might mess up and say too much, she stopped herself and tried to stay quiet throughout the rest of the meal.

"Thank you, Annie and Ernie, for a night to remember. Great stories, great food, and well-done on the secrecy, buddy," offered her dad.

"Hey, Brooke Lynn, need to get your pup. Let's say our goodbyes," her mother said.

She felt a sudden closeness she hadn't felt in months with Mike. It was nice to see him so happy.

"What a night, Mike! My dad said our fathers were super close as kids growing up. They've been friends forever. Do you think we'll still be best friends when we are as old as them?" Brooke Lynn reflected.

"Of course, no matter what, we'll be BFFs."

Mike gave her a light push. She giggled at his friendly touch.

Chapter Twenty-Two

GIRLIE FUN

Brooke Lynn's excitement was at an all-time high with the thought of hanging out with her besties today. She had thought she may feel awkward and worry about the day, but things felt different – she was closer to Mike than she had been for a while, and the break in the rain helped her mood. An unexpected flutter moved in her tummy as she listened to Mike's message. Had the once-familiar voice mildly cracked mid-sentence?

Growing pangs… his voice is changing.

"Forgot to mention that I heard back from the orthodontist and, well, guess what? I am getting braces. I'm okay with it because I'm sick of my overbite. Like you said, I'll be done with them before we go onto high school. Thanks for the positive thought. It helped. See you later."

Brooke Lynn shot him a fast text. Her pal was taking the news well.

"T+ ☺ CU @ 3."

She was antsy to close *The Case of the Hidden Shoe*. If they could just figure out *who* owns the fancy Italian shoe!

It was clear to her time was not on their side. The push of activity and increased traffic through the neighborhood indicated the first home would be ready before the party deadline. And the newly hired security guard was one more person to avoid. He could be part of a celebrity's bodyguard team.

I bet it's a Hollywood actor!

Instead of rushing around, it felt nice to take an extra minute or two to look more put-together. Brooke Lynn had made this conscious decision after talking with Susie. Selecting one of her newer outfits, she chose the red cropped pants with a navy crewneck sweater with sparkly accent dots around the neckline, which she adored.

When she posed in the full-length mirror, her unruly, fly-away hair got her attention. Besides the staticky strands, the cowlick on the back of her head wouldn't lay flat. It just went sideways. Right then, her mom walked in.

Figures!

"Almost ready? Ah, do you want some help? Remember when I used to pull your hair up just so…?"

Her mother gathered a big handful from each side of her head pulling it taut. She snatched the barrette off the dresser and readily clasped it. With a dab of gel in her palms, she gave the strands a rough brushing with her fingers. The static disappeared.

"Ta da! Beautiful. Pulled back, it shows off your sweet face." Her mother beamed.

Really, Mom? Do you think I'm still eight years old!?!

Brooke Lynn held back on rolling her eyes at her mother's goofy praise. She wasn't good at accepting compliments, especially when they made her feel like a little girl.

Her mother passed the hand-held mirror to Brooke Lynn. The mother-of-pearl handle felt smooth. It gave her the ability to see the back of her head.

Why haven't I used this more often?

As she held it firmly while turning to the front view, Brooke Lynn made a funny, snarly face at her reflection. They both giggled. It had been a while since they had shared a laugh.

"I gave you this silver barrette on your last birthday. Probably time to get some more accessories since your hair is getting longer.

Maybe for your birthday coming in a few weeks. Still can't believe you'll be 12," her mom mused.

"Much better, Mom. Thanks. I'm not sure I can do it on my own, but it looks nice," Brooke Lynn said.

The front doorbell chimed indicating Susie had arrived.

"I can help you any time, you know. You look nice by the way," her mother revealed.

"Susie and I'll be outside waiting in the car."

"I'll be just a sec."

Brooke Lynn gave one lasting look in the mirror and with an approving nod, she trotted to catch up.

After what seemed like way too many changing rooms with multiple outfits at the store, Brooke Lynn finally decided on two spiffy pants and two knit tops. It was time to head upstairs to the intimate apparel department. Her mother wandered over to the perfume counter leaving the two girls to hang out alone.

"Meet you two back over here in an hour," her mother said.

Susie pulled three bra options for her friend and handed them to her already loaded arms. Brooke Lynn decided on some possible underwear choices to try on.

"Here you go. Try these and if you need more styles or sizes, just holler. Do you want me to come into the dressing room with you?"

Brooke Lynn's eyes darted off to the side in a modest blush and shook her head in a negative fashion. She wanted to see how they looked on her own.

"If I have any questions, Susie, I'll holler. Thanks though."

Brooke Lynn undressed and timidly stood in front of the mirror topless with just her underpants on. Pleased at how her body was developing curves, she critically eyed the high-rise cotton briefs.

These underpants need to go!

CHAPTER TWENTY-THREE

MIRROR-MIRROR

Standing up straight, Brooke Lynn sucked in her middle and lifted her chest. She pivoted sideways, then back to the front and once again from the other side. It was the first time she had seen herself naked in stark bright lighting... with a three-way mirror to boot!

When did my chest go from two flat pancakes to rising mini muffins?

She digested her image for a second more. No wonder she was beginning to feel different! She stood up on her tiptoes and twirled once before landing flat-footed. Annoyed, she shook her head.

Shrugging off her mild modesty, she picked up the first option, a white training bra. After fastening it, she tilted her head just so and realized she wasn't impressed with the stretchy, flimsy material.

Taking it off, she grabbed the lacy underwire push up bra. A bit awkwardly, she managed to wrap it around, hooking both spots and jiggled her small breasts inside each cup for adjustment. Stepping back, she moved her arms above her head and felt a tight pull around the rib cage. It was digging in near her armpit. Nope, not this one either. Her bosoms didn't fill out the small cups anyway and she wasn't about to stuff her bra to make it work! Disappointment started creeping in. She unhooked it.

Just about ready to give up, she looked at the last choice, the sports bra. Sitting scrunched and shapeless, it was a size Petite Small but practical. With a roll of her eyes, hoping this one would be the one, she slipped it over her head. She wiggled and squirmed into it until it sat in the right places. It was perfect! It offered enough coverage with minor lift and it was comfortable.

After trying on the rest of her garments, including a pair of low-rise undies, Brooke Lynn was about to exit when she heard the whispers.

"I was talking to his wife and she said he's thinking of purchasing a home over there. Do you think they're the secret homebuyers?" In the next changing room over, voices of two ladies reached Brooke Lynn's ears. She listened.

"Well, I talked to Mr. Colby at school last week. He said he and his wife had a brief discussion about the new homes but they hadn't decided yet. So, I don't know," said the second voice.

Brooke Lynn rushed out with clothes in tow. She had to tell Susie the rumor. She couldn't believe they had been talking about Mr. Colby.

"Susie, I just overheard some ladies in the changing room talking about The Colbys, like they might be the first homeowners. That's juicy stuff, huh?"

"Yeah, the rumors are everywhere. One minute it's a celeb, and the next it's somebody's neighbor. I've been hoping to see someone famous while shopping, but nothing so far. We'll just have to wait," Susie answered. "I hope it *is* a celebrity like my mom thinks though and not boring Mr. Colby!"

"I don't know…" Brooke Lynn wanted to speak to Mike to tell him what she'd heard. She glanced down at the clothing in her hands. "So, the two bras didn't work at all for me but the sports bra, well, it's the most comfortable. Let me grab two more as backup. I think it will help me feel less self-conscious. Oh, and the two outfits you helped me pick out are so cute. And check out these new panties. More of a grownup style, yeah? It's all about the comfort, Susie," Brooke Lynn said.

"Glad you found something that works. I even grabbed two sports bras for myself. I'm the opposite of you. I need it for gym class to hold everything in! I picked up a new top too. Do you like it? It was on the sale rack," Susie asked, showing Brooke Lynn a V-neck creamy colored long-sleeved blouse. It wasn't her style but she knew it would look terrific on her bestie.

"It's pretty, Susie. It looks see-through though. You'll need a camisole. You have such a good eye for clothes. Do you get your ideas from magazines?"

Suddenly, Brooke Lynn felt impish standing in the middle of the lingerie area. She moved toward the cashier.

"I'm a bit obsessed. You've seen all my fashion magazines lying around. It's a dream of mine to one day get into the fashion field," Susie responded. Brooke Lynn wondered why she hadn't noticed it before or they hadn't shared this dream together. They were changing and getting their own interests.

At just 8 years old and starting 3rd grade, Susie was the newbie at Santa Mesa Elementary School. What started as a slight stutter soon became emphasized during the transition to a new school. At the same time, while Mike was recovering from heart surgery, Brooke Lynn's social awkwardness intensified. She was lost without her sidekick. Drawn to each other by their shortfalls, their sisterly bond was instant. Susie's speech therapy was in full session while Brooke Lynn's friendship void had been filled. A bit of an odd couple, they had been there for each other through lots of ups and downs.

They snickered when they found Brooke Lynn's mother trying on sunglasses. It looked like the counter had been overtaken by the entire selection from the display case. They watched from a distance until she looked up finally.

"Hey, are you girls all done? Want to grab a cone at Hammond's Ice Cream Shoppe around the corner for old-time sake? It feels warmer today – perfect for a scoop or two. What do you say?"

"Sure!" they answered together.

It was turning out to be a terrific day. Brooke Lynn embraced it.

"Mrs. Gale, I need to be home about noon. I promised my mother I'd help with watching Jimmy for a while. Can we go home right after ice cream?" Susie asked.

"Of course, we can get it to-go instead of sitting down in the shop. Where'd the time go? Seems like it was just 10:00 and it's already going on noon. Next time we go shopping, we'll plan a bit more time so I can take you girls to lunch too."

As they headed for ice cream, Brooke Lynn saw a flyer for the Oak Grove party in the window of a shop. A group of girls were gathered around it. She caught some of their conversation and nudged Susie.

"You hear those girls? They think their friend's aunt spotted a celebrity over at the development last week! Geez, so much gossip in town. Everyone's curious but no one seems to know for sure," Brooke Lynn said.

"Yeah, just like my mom seeing that famous actor. Right?" Susie laughed.

Brooke Lynn couldn't imagine a better girlfriend than Susie. She wished she didn't feel disloyal to her when hanging out with Mike. They were complete opposites, but she enjoyed the variety of both her friends.

Yet she couldn't get rid of the conflicted feeling… like she was somehow caught in the middle.

Chapter Twenty-Four

SUSIE ON SITE

Mrs. Gale called out to Susie's mom perched on the front steps. The sun streamed over Mrs. Reynolds' covered shoulders giving her a youthful glow. Seated next to her was Jimmy, her eight-year-old son, who was busying himself with a blue toy dinosaur.

"Hi, Rita, hi, Jimmy. Hope we didn't keep Susie too long?"

"No, Sally, I just hope my daughter didn't spend too much of her allowance." Susie's mother laughed.

Rita Reynolds was a petite woman with a full figure for her tiny size. Although only casual acquaintances, they had remained friendly over the years. Mrs. Reynolds, widowed at the young age of 27, worked long hours at the restaurant. She recently helped open the new eatery, *Ceci's Salad Bar*, as the manager.

Mrs. Gale waved goodbye after unloading Susie's packages from the trunk.

"Every time I see Rita, it reminds me that we should try Ceci Hardiman's new restaurant," her mom mused as they drove away. "Did you get everything you needed? You two seemed to be having a good time. She's always pleasant."

"That's why she's my best girlfriend. She's real patient and always supportive. All the girlie stuff comes naturally to her… me? Not so much, Mom. And yeah, I picked up two new outfits with my allowance, plus a couple of sports bras and some undies. Do you think I'm what they call a late bloomer?"

Lightly chuckling as though absorbed in her own memory, her mother looked at her daughter with a sincerity.

"Oh, I don't think you're late for anything. Everybody grows and matures at a different pace, including me at your age. You'll start noticing more physical changes along with emotional growth spurts, well, that's what my mother called them. But, Brooke, it happens organically, and it can't be forced… it's all very natural. Susie just happened to blossom early which doesn't mean you're late… you're just right. You know you can ask me anything, right? Okay, help me carry in some of these packages," her mother requested.

"Yeah, I know. Hey, Mom, I want to reorganize my closet sometime this weekend with my new things and get rid of some old clothes for the donation pile," Brooke said as they carried in packages. "And I want to rearrange my bedroom too. Is it okay if I move my bed up against the other wall so I can look out the window from my bed? Promise I won't scuff the floor. I can ask Arnie to help me."

"I hadn't thought about your bed being there, but it makes sense. Sure. Change is good… maybe we'll pick up some fun things for your room too. Spiff it up."

"When I was at Susie's, she had a pink furry pillow on her couch. Super cool and cute! I think a couple of bright pillows would be perfect for my bedroom. Maybe some fun things for my walls too," Brooke said, fixing herself a PB&J sandwich.

"Sounds like a plan. Why don't you take Samantha Sue to the park today with Susie and Mike? She could use the exercise," her mom suggested.

"Oh… er, okay," Brooke Lynn said reluctantly.

Brooke Lynn didn't want to tell her Mom the truth about where she was meeting her friends. She just wanted to close the case. One more visit onto the site surely wouldn't hurt anything, right?

Meeting up with her friends as planned, they made the climb up the road with Sam in tow. When Mike and Susie started chatting about their classmates, she felt left out… again. Annoyed, she walked ahead. She glanced back to see if Susie was trying to impress Mike.

Brooke Lynn felt like the third wheel... like *she* was tagging along instead of Susie!

She stopped at the top of the hill and noted the gate was open. Her sleuth instincts were aroused. She'd need to keep Samantha Sue quiet just in case the guard was lurking around. Brooke Lynn interrupted her chums chatting.

"It amazes me how fast the homes are coming along. Let's keep our voices down in case the security guard is making his rounds," Brooke Lynn stated.

"Will do. It *all* looks amazing to me. They are so big. Just hope I don't get my nice shoes dirty," Susie said worried.

"See that one over there? That's the one Mike and I have already explored. It's pretty cool," Brooke Lynn said, pointing.

This was their opportunity to get closure on *The Case of the Hidden Shoe*. They walked around the backside first. Brooke Lynn jiggled the door, but it was locked.

"Darn it! Well, this is frustrating. It doesn't look like we'll be able to go inside. You can at least peek in the windows, Susie!" Brooke Lynn said.

Susie didn't budge. She stared down at the uneven gravel and muddy soil like she was waiting for a better suggestion.

"Well, let's try the front of the house to see if any of those doors are open. Wouldn't want to get your shoes soiled," Brooke Lynn snipped.

Why am I mocking my best girlfriend?

"Really, Brooke Lynn!?!" Susie snapped back.

Mike moved ahead of the girls to the next door. He was ignoring their remarks. He grabbed the handle, but it was also locked. As they turned the corner, Brooke Lynn volunteered defeat.

"Well, looks pretty buttoned up. Maybe it's getting too close to the party, you know, finishing up last-minute stuff. Guess you waited too long to get a peek, Susie. You snooze, you lose," Brooke Lynn teased.

This whole thing felt off. Brooke Lynn guessed having Susie with them was a mistake. She felt like a lousy friend.

Chapter Twenty-Five

TWO SLEUTHS AND SAM

"I don't know why you're talking to me like this, Brooke Lynn! We had a lovely time shopping. *You're* the one who said Saturday would be a good time to come. We could have made it earlier in the week!" Susie cried.

"I'm just stating the obvious. You should have come prepared by wearing some old shoes. It *is* still under construction, Susie. You'll just have to wait until the party," Brooke Lynn replied.

Remembering there was one more door around the other corner of the house, Brooke Lynn didn't say a peep. She sensed Mike wasn't too keen on having Susie there either… maybe?

"Yeah, well, I thought there would be grass, maybe a walkway around the house. And I wanted to tell my mom all about it. Well, that's-that then. I'm out of here. Bye!" Susie declared, flouncing away from the house and towards the gates.

"Now that she's gone, geez, it felt different having Susie with us. Not in a bad way, just…well, she can be a pain," Brooke Lynn said, letting out a long sigh. "I think she was more concerned about her shoes getting dirty than exploring."

"Hey, come on, she's okay. I kind of know what you mean when she didn't want to mess up her shoes, but no biggie," he said, smirking.

"I know she likes to look neat, but really? She's so prissy sometimes," Brooke Lynn said.

She knew she was being two-faced but the ranting kind of felt good. Noticing Mike's scowl, she switched the conversation to a more upbeat note.

"Mike, don't get me wrong, I like her as a friend, I'm just frustrated I guess."

Selfishly, Brooke Lynn was glad it was just the two of them. Maybe they could finish their investigation. She tugged on the leash for Sam to stay in step.

"I think there's one last door on the side of the garage. Up for trying it?" Brooke Lynn asked.

"Sure thing."

Mike approached the door, jiggled it a bit and this time, voila! He adjusted his small backpack before entering. The stowed heavy-duty flashlight may come in handy.

"Well, what do you know?" Brooke Lynn said slyly.

Once inside the garage, Mike located three doors. Two turned out to be storage rooms.

"There, I think that's the one leading to the laundry room and then into the main area of the house. Remember?"

Turning the knob, Mike stepped inside. Staying a few steps behind with Samantha Sue, Brooke Lynn thought she saw a shadow in the corner window peeking in. She gasped. Had Susie come back after all?

Mike started nosing around cabinets, looking for any clues. He was unaware of Susie's presence. Brooke Lynn side-stepped up to the dust-coated pane. Too late. All she spotted was the back of her friend running down the hill.

I'll bet Susie's mad at me!

"Find anything? Hey, maybe we should have tried *all* the doors while Susie was here? Then she could have seen inside too," Brooke Lynn asked, feeling guilty about not suggesting it earlier. She had known about the door.

Mike shrugged, and Brooke Lynn shook Susie from her mind. She had to focus on why they were here – her curiosity about the red stained shoe soon overshadowed her remorse about Susie missing out.

"Okay, let's check on the shoe. Then we're out of here. I have to get Sam home," Brooke Lynn suggested.

As they walked down the hallway, Mike's flashlight allowed them to move faster. He entered the last room on the left. Samantha Sue scampered ahead.

"Found it! Someone knows it's here though. It's been moved out of the cubby. Scoot, Sam," Mike commanded.

After sniffing around, Samantha Sue retreated towards Brooke Lynn. With the high beam on the shoe, it was certain. The shoe had been moved out from the darkened corner.

"We still don't know *who* this belongs to or *if* that's blood, but why did they decide to leave it behind?" Brooke Lynn mused. "Hey, wouldn't it be so funny if someone is wearing these shoes at the grand opening party? We'd soon know who it belongs to!"

Just as they were exiting the room, the flashlight shined on something behind the door. Brooke Lynn snatched up the small piece of paper.

"SFO, Flt 2162, Seat 14B. Maybe the secret client of Mr. Clemens dropped this. I think it's part of a plane ticket stub. No name though. I'll bet his client is from out-of-town and someone famous. That's why it's such a big mystery. I'll look up the info," Brooke Lynn suggested.

"Maybe it's a clue? We'd better get going. I'm not sure if we'll ever figure this bloody shoe thing out. It probably doesn't matter anyway," Mike stated glumly.

"What do you mean it doesn't matter? We need to finish the case. Sometimes you can be so negative," she said.

"It's not that. I want to finish the case too…"

"Then why are you being so negative?" Brooke Lynn asked, trying not to sound frustrated.

"Well… I overheard my dad on the phone talking to some company in Texas about a job. It's got me worried… like what if his new job is somewhere else? I don't want to move."

"He'll find something here. I know my dad's firm is hiring. So, don't worry yet," Brooke Lynn said, more to reassure herself than him. This was *not* good news. She'd hate it if her pal had to move away. Her friend finally has his dad home, but what if it's only temporary?

"Okay, I'll try to stay positive. And you need to get your pup home. Plus, my dad has some chores for me. See you, BL and Sam," he said, waving goodbye.

She waved back, skipping along with Sam, and her mind wandered to Susie. Brooke Lynn thought about her having returned to the house and catching them inside. Guilt filled her mind. She needed to mend their friendship soon, but then more guilt swept in; she hadn't even thought about her homework!

Diving into her homework before supper, Brooke Lynn rummaged through her bookbag. She pulled out the latest reading assignment. The first chapter of the story had her stumped. She re-read the same paragraph four times. Tossing it aside, she checked her phone for a message from Susie. Nothing. Instead of calling Susie, Brooke Lynn jumped at the sight of Mike's new text.

"URGNT, LITE ON @ HOUSE AGN, R U N? MT^ @ 8."

The image of Susie staring through the window returned. Ugh! It conflicted with her excitement about Mike's message. Brooke Lynn checked again for a message from Susie. Maybe she hadn't seen them inside the house?

Wishful thinking! I'll bet she's good and mad.

Her conscience won. She knew she needed to set the record straight with Susie first… Mike could wait.

Chapter Twenty-Six

COULD SPELL TROUBLE

"It's another great day! You know what to do at the beep," Susie's voicemail greeting said.

"Hi, Susie, I thought I saw you at the site after you left… did you come back? Well, anyway, Mike and I found one last door that was unlocked. It was a fluke. Hope you're not mad and I'm sorry. I'll call you tomorrow after my chores. Talk more then," Brooke Lynn recorded.

Susie phoned right back, catching Brooke Lynn by surprise. She let her talk.

"Yeah, Brooke Lynn, it was me looking in the window. I was mad when I saw you and Mike inside. It felt like you didn't want me there," Susie said, then took a deep breath. "But I shouldn't have stormed off. I'm sorry for leaving in a huff, and I'm glad I got a bit of a look inside through the windows – you're right, the house looks great. I'm glad you left me a message; I've been worrying about things."

"Me too and yeah, I'm sorry for being short with you. I've been a little on edge myself," Brooke Lynn explained, but felt relieved. "I'm glad things are okay between us though. I'll see you later."

Susie had been a good friend, so it felt better clearing up that situation before it festered. Now onto her next challenging friend… she texted Mike.

"TTLY BUT NOT ☹," Brooke Lynn responded.

She couldn't believe he was asking her to sneak out again. Her instincts said not to go. But part of her enjoyed taking the risk with

Mike even if it was daring. Brooke Lynn walked into the family room. The sense of feeling grownup after dealing with Susie faded as she stood in front of her folks.

"Good night," she softly said.

Her parents looked sweet sitting next to each other on the sectional as though on a Date Night. Her mother kept her focus on the screen.

"Good night, Brooke Lynn."

She pretended to go upstairs, listened for a second, and then walked out the side door quietly. Once again, the guilt was jabbing at her, but she wanted to get this over with even if it was sneaky.

The entry gate was open.

Hmm? Maybe when it is open, people are on the premises. Or could the guard have forgotten to lock it?

Brooke Lynn hunched down low over the handlebars heeding to caution.

After pedaling straight to the first house, the cameo of Mike's head poking out from the side reminded her to be extra vigilant. In the driveway was Mr. Clemens' old clunker. Without saying a word, she parked her bike next to Mike's. They walked to the back, edging their way in the shadows toward the middle of the home.

Right before they peeked in the window, Brooke Lynn looked for the trash cans. There were none in the vicinity. Still unable to make out the faces, the hushed voices were the same. It was Mr. Clemens and the same male voice they'd heard before – the voice that belonged to his client.

"Let's see if we can see them better from the other window," Brooke Lynn whispered.

They moved deliberately over the gravel in the darkened back yard to the next window, but they were unsuccessful. It was a more restrictive view.

"Let's try one more window - the one on the way far end. It's risky so let's hurry." Mike's eyes brightened.

"Okay, I'll follow you this time," Brooke Lynn replied.

They strained to see through the next window, but the two men were standing too far away and off to one side of the room.

"It was worth a try. Sorry, I was hoping we could close the case once and for all. If we could just see them," Mike admitted sadly.

They went back the way they came into the back yard. Hearing a door swing wide open, they jumped behind one of the freshly planted evergreens. They waited painfully, unable to get a clear shot.

"Everything looks all set, Tim," the quieter male voice said.

"Great then, I'll call you next week for another walk-through," Mr. Clemens responded.

The suspicious male had called Mr. Clemens by his first name. Chums perhaps? Shortly after, the men left the back yard. As they heard the car drive away, Mike crawled out from behind the oversized bush. His legs were cramped from squatting for what seemed like an hour. After declaring it was safe for Brooke Lynn to come out too, Mike pointed to the wall on the other side of the yard.

"Head toward our bikes. Stay crouched low so the security guard won't see us. You go first this time," Mike suggested.

Brooke Lynn led the way – no more spilled trash cans if she could help it! She rounded the corner with Mike trailing and stopped. She spotted the blood-stained shoe straight ahead. Directly in front of her – about six feet away – was **The Shoe!**

What the heck… why is it outside?

Her eyes darted sideways another couple of inches and realized the mate was sitting next to it. As she looked directly above the shoes, she saw a pair of legs attached to the shoes. She bit her lip and swallowed. Somebody was wearing them! Standing right in front of them in the shadow, half hidden from view was… she adjusted her eyes to the changing light.

Can it be?

A man was apparently wearing not only the red-stained shoe but *both* shoes!

Scared speechless, no words came out of her mouth. Unsure what to do next, Brooke Lynn somehow managed to spring up from her crouched position to face the shadow. Right before she could warn Mike, the man stepped from the darkened area into the hazy moonlight.

In that split second, she froze.

Chapter Twenty-Seven
BUSTED

An ultimate disbelief took over. Brooke Lynn, now breathing rapidly, turned her head down toward Mike. Ascending from his knelt position, they stood side-by-side. The two young sleuths knew they were busted. The steady trickle of fear took over. It ran across Brooke Lynn's stiffened back.

The man inched closer. He looked at the two 7th graders with a surprised, yet stern expression. Shaking his head back and forth, they could tell they were in trouble. Big trouble!

"Hi, ah – er – um, Dad?" Mike stuttered.

He glanced at Brooke Lynn for backup. She'd let Mike take the lead.

"Hi there, son, what on earth is going on here?!" Mr. Larkin asked.

He patiently waited for a response, rapidly tapping his foot while unfolding his crossed arms. Brooke Lynn stared straight ahead at Mr. Larkin, not daring to open her mouth.

"What are you doing here, Michael? Cat got your tongue, huh? Does your mother know you are here? And do you know what time it is?!" Ernie Larkin continued.

Mike's eyes darted back and forth between his dad and Brooke Lynn.

"Ur, well, Dad, we, uh, I noticed the light on when Mom and I came home earlier. I wanted to check out who might be in the house this late. So, I texted Brooke Lynn to meet me here. You see, Dad, we've been watching the construction progress as the Two Keepers of the neighborhood. We've been protecting the neighborhood."

It sounded lame as he said it. Mike was rambling and his buddy was no help. Mike looked down at his dad's shoes realizing they were the same pair as Mr. Clemens'. His dad's shoe had a visible yet faded spot on it.

Trying to put all the pieces of the puzzle together quickly, Mike was glad it was his dad's shoes, and not some bad person's. But then he became even more mixed up.

"Dad, wait, those old shoes you're wearing, they're your shoes? Then why does Mr. Clemens have the same shoes?"

"Wait, wait, hold on... too many questions. Alright, what is *really* going on here, Mike? I think you'd better slow down and explain what *you* are doing here after we told you to stay away from the construction area. And why are you so concerned about my shoes?" his dad demanded.

Mike continued trying his best not to sound irrational.

"When we saw the blood stain, I mean, the red-stained shoe left in the room the other day, well, we kept checking on the house in case someone had gotten injured or something bad was going on. We saw the stain on the floor in the back room too. We kept checking back to see if someone would claim the stained shoe. But now that you are wearing them... wait, why was your shoe here, Dad? Nothing makes sense. And when did you drive up? We didn't see your truck."

Mike became frustrated with his inability to explain himself or understand what was going on. He exhaled in a defeated huff.

"Calm down, son. First off, the shoe was stained by a spilled paint can while visiting with Mr. Clemens. I hadn't seen him in a long time and wanted to ask how you were doing in school. He handed me a paint can he was holding while he reached into his briefcase for your student record. Well, that's when the can slipped out of my hands. What a mess! It's not blood, son, no. Geez, I asked Joe, the manager, if he had some paint remover to clean the stain off so I wouldn't track any of it home. He texted me earlier today to let me know I could pick it up this evening. I'm parked on the other side where Joe said he'd leave the shoe. You two are the last people I thought I'd run into here," Mr. Larkin said.

With bikes loaded, Mr. Larkin further explained while they rode home. Brooke Lynn looked at her watch. It was almost 10:00! No sneaking back in tonight. She sunk further into the front seat, wishing she were invisible.

"I've known Mr. Clemens for years. He was stationed with me overseas, and when he retired last year, we kept in touch. He said he had finally gotten a teaching job and it just so happened to be in Santa Mesa. Then he emailed that you were going to be in his class this year. What was the likelihood? I asked him to do me a favor and send me updates about your progress. By the way, your teacher also has a real estate license and does this on the side. Enough about that... about you two sneaking out tonight, well, that's another story," Mr. Larkin said.

"Dad, Mr. C. was here earlier but he left with some guy, maybe the mystery homeowner. They took off a while ago. Wait, that's why he has the same Italian shoes? He was overseas with you?"

"Yeah, we bought our shoes on an assignment we had in Italy a few years back. They'll be plenty of time to talk. First things first, you are going to have to understand the consequences of sneaking out and being in a restricted area."

Mr. Larkin's truck pulled into The Gale's driveway. The lights were still on inside her house.

"Brooke Lynn, you'd better run along inside before your mother has all of our heads. I won't lie for you; I suggest you walk in and tell them right away. Oops – too late – here comes your dad!"

Mr. Larkin let out a low sigh as he rolled down his window. Looking inside the cab and then in the truck bed where the bikes were laying, Mr. Gale shook his head.

"Hey, Ernie, what's going on? Oh, I see… Brooke Lynn Gale, come on inside! Thanks for dropping her off. I'll call you tomorrow."

Mr. Gale hoisted his daughter's bike out of the truck bed. She wheeled it to the side of the garage dreading what was about to happen. Her mom's frown and crossed arms signaled she was upset. Brooke Lynn wasn't expecting a hug.

"We were worried when we noticed you weren't in your room a few minutes ago," her mother said, her voice icy. "I'm glad you are safe but let's start from the beginning, you have some explaining to do."

"Really, I'm fine, Mom. Stop making it more than it is," Brooke Lynn snapped.

A bit embarrassed at her parent's reaction, the tween wanted to crawl into a dark hole and never come out. Her conscience stopped her though and her more mature side won. She saw the looks of disappointment and worry on her parents' faces and, just like with Susie earlier, she knew it was time to set things right with her parents.

"Okay, let me explain…" her apology was underway.

Chapter Twenty-Eight
GROUNDED

Lying in bed as the low light streamed through her white curtains, Brooke Lynn's head started spinning. The thought of facing her parents this morning felt heavy. The worst feeling of conflict came over her like a gut-wrenching pit in her stomach. Memorizing every speckled spot on the ceiling, she held her stare, replaying last night's events.

If only we hadn't gotten caught.

Now, she was grounded. A whole week on restriction! She buried her head in her pillow. She was mad at herself. Conflicted, she remembered her parents' strained faces as she explained her lame reasoning for sneaking out.

No phone privileges, no investigations or hanging out with friends for one *long* week! And the worst thing… getting her parents' trust back. It would be a slow crawl out of the doghouse.

Prior to going downstairs, Brooke Lynn looked around and decided today was the day for cleaning up her room. Getting into her new routine, into action.

Time for a change.

Reaching for her phone instinctively to text Mike, she pulled her hand back to her side. Ugh – no phone privileges. She was curious about his punishment but had no way to communicate. She fumed.

Shaking those thoughts away, she looked at her desktop. Her to-do list sat in the center. But first, she decided to clarify something with Susie that had been nagging her. Since she couldn't call or text, Brooke Lynn grabbed her favorite purple pen and some note paper.

Hi Susie,

Sorry I haven't texted or called. Saturday night I snuck out to meet up with Mike at the Oak Grove site. Like a dummy, I went. We got caught. I'm <u>grounded for one whole week</u>! No phone or anything until next Saturday.

There's something that's been on my mind lately... not sure how to say this, so I'll just come right out with it. Do YOU like Mike as in LIKE-LIKE him?

When you tutored him the other day, that kind of bugged me. He usually comes to me with any school problems.

And then you said he had gotten "a lot cuter."

When you wanted to come with us to the housing project, it felt weird because you've never asked before to hang out with Mike. It's cool if that's what you want, but it feels strange.

Well, that's all I had on my mind. Can we talk about this at lunch break?

Miss you lots,

BL

Brooke Lynn stuffed the note in an envelope. She felt better now that she had written her honest feelings to her best girlfriend. She didn't want to be two-faced or disloyal to her... it was time to just get it all out. She placed it into her bookbag to pass to Susie soon, hopefully.

She slowly made the dreaded walk downstairs for breakfast. The kitchen was empty with a note on the kitchen table. She felt her shoulders relax.

Brooke Lynn,

Went to the grocery store with your father, and then run a few errands. Be home later this morning. Arnie left for practice.

X Mom

After eating some cereal, Brooke Lynn chased her dog around the back yard for half an hour or so, tossing her a tennis ball.

"Got to go in, girl, and start on my chores. We'll play more later."

On the top of her to-do list – clean out closet. Today was the day to organize! Maybe she'd even rearrange her bedroom furniture if she could snag Arnie. She got a burst of energy at the thought of a fresh new look to her bedroom.

When Arnie walked by about an hour later, he poked his head into his sister's room. Brooke Lynn was tidying the top shelf of her closet. Her bed was halfway out from the wall.

"What are you up to, sis? Moving things around in here? Want me to help you move the bed?" he offered, lifting the frame slightly. "Where to?"

"Oh, you scared me for a sec. Great, what a big help and just in the nick of time," Brooke Lynn said, feeling lucky for his offer.

Arnie gave one last shove, and his sister signaled her approval with a thumbs up.

"That ought to do it. I've wanted my bed against this wall for a while now so I could wake up looking out the window. See what I mean?"

They both stood back and looked over the new set up. Brooke Lynn turned to her brother, determined to have an adult conversation this time. No fights.

"Hey, Arnie, in case no one told you, I got grounded last night. I snuck out with Mike. We wanted to check out the first house at the site because Mike saw lights on late last night. We went snooping around but got caught by Mr. Gale. He had to pick something up over there and found us nosing about. It was ugly… so busted. Anyway, I thought I'd let you know – one week on restriction."

"Oh yeah, sis? I never thought you'd do anything that outlandish. Just so you don't feel too bad, I've been on restriction before for staying out too late myself. It'll all pass before you know it. Hey, good eye on choosing this angle for the bed. Let me know if you need any other pieces moved," he said.

"I think I'm all done for now. Thanks a bunch – really appreciate it," Brooke Lynn said flashing him a smile.

He glanced at her with a look she had never seen from him; it was one of acceptance as though they shared a common battle scar. She didn't feel like the goody-two-shoes any longer. Plus, they had managed to get along for more than five minutes. It was like she had climbed over a hurdle with her sibling.

"Okay, later then. Oh, have you heard any news on *who* the new homeowner is at the development?" Arnie asked. "Belinda keeps asking me if I've heard. She's caught up in the rumors about a celebrity or something. I wondered, with all your snooping, maybe you'd figured it out."

"I'm stumped too. Not a peep in class either. Some are guessing it's someone famous or from out-of-town. Let you know if I hear anything," she answered.

Brooke Lynn grinned while standing in the middle of her bedroom. She wrapped one arm over the other and hugged herself. She felt happy with the change and had enjoyed having some time with her brother – he'd spent such a lot of time in his room, with his girlfriend or staring at his phone recently.

Hearing her mother's footsteps coming upstairs, the knot in her belly returned.

Please, say something nice.

Chapter Twenty-Nine
ROOM FOR MOM

"Hey there, oh, you're right, Brooke Lynn," her mother said when she saw her room. "The bed does look fantastic there and the bookcase is better on that wall too. You got your brother to help, huh? How'd your closet turn out?"

"Everything is organized by pants and tops for school, then hanging around clothes on this side. Sweaters are on top. Oh, and that's the donation pile. I like it a lot. It feels good too. Arnie was super helpful." Brooke Lynn grinned.

"Excellent job! Maybe I should have you do my closet. Hey, want to come with me to Mel's Home Goods in a few? I need to pick up some new placemats for the kitchen table and a couple of odds and ends. You mentioned you wanted some knick-knacks and pillows for the new look."

"I guess? I didn't know if you were still mad at me or if I would be allowed to go out except for school. I feel bad you were worried, Mom. But yeah, I did want a couple of things to finish off my room."

It beats being bored.

"I'm not happy about you sneaking out but we have to move on. Going with me doesn't change anything about your restriction. I'd enjoy the company and thought you'd like to get out of the house for a bit."

"Yeah, I get it. I'm really liking the upbeat feel in here now. It's more my style and getting a few pillows will finish it off perfectly!"

Brooke Lynn placed both hands on her hips. She felt older in a good way after last night's rocky event.

"You know, I did the same thing when I was your age; rearranging the furniture and personalizing the room to make it my domain – my own space. Okay, if you're going to come, be ready in 15 minutes. Did you get enough info about the project for your essay paper?" her mom asked.

"Pretty much, except you had mentioned the town was still concerned about some items. Any word?" Brooke Lynn responded.

"Just remind me later tonight, I'll call Annie Larkin. She said the planning group would have some answers later today after they vote."

As Brooke Lynn listened to her mother explain the process between the developer and planning group on the ride back home after shopping, she felt inspired. Getting some kids together to focus on community improvements would be a good idea.

"I think I'd like to get more involved in local affairs. Maybe even set up a youth group so the town could hear from the kids' perspective. We understand more than adults realize. I'll talk to Miss Hart about it," Brooke Lynn pondered.

"Yeah, getting input from the local kids and bringing the ideas to the planning group would offer some fresh points of view. I'm pleased you find it interesting," her mother agreed.

They pulled into the driveway and spotted Samantha Sue standing up on her two hind legs peering out the bay window. They stared up at their pooch's nose pressed against the fogged glass. That cozy shared moment was confirmed by her mother's cheerful remark.

"Looks like Sam's happy we're home!"

Brooke Lynn was glad they were home too, despite being grounded, she was excited to finish her room with the pillows they'd bought.

Chapter Thirty

CLASS SPEECHES

Monday had finally arrived, and Brooke Lynn couldn't wait until it was over!

Essay time - yikes!

Brooke Lynn was heading out the door when her mom called out from the kitchen.

"Good news, Brooke, you'd gone to bed already when the call came in last night. Mrs. Larkin said the vote was unanimous - the developer agreed to *all* the outstanding concerns. Good news, huh?"

Brooke Lynn ran over and hugged her mother. Her class would be happy to hear this news. Maybe that would calm her nerves.

She was wrong. The tension in the air was apparent the minute she stepped into the classroom. Everyone was antsy, not just Brooke Lynn.

Prepared but still unsettled, Brooke Lynn listened to her fellow classmates recite each of their stories. When it was her turn, she stood up after loosening her stuck thighs from the chair. Yuck-o!

As she walked up to the front table, her hands felt damp. The term paper shook in her tight grip. Looking out at the sea of faces, she hoped no one noticed her shaky hands. When her tummy started doing flip-flops, she swallowed hard, then drew in a deep breath to begin.

"Hi everyone. Being Open Minded, by Brooke Lynn Gale…"

Somewhere in the middle, she forgot all about the uneasiness. The sentences sailed off her tongue as she neared the end.

"...and the final vote was all in favor to save the old oak trees along the property at Oak Grove Park, including the picnic area. The hiking trails and bike paths have guaranteed open access year-round. The planning group had made an impact on Santa Mesa's future by being open-minded about the new development. The increased homes meant additional families would be able to move into the area. To curb the congestion, they agreed to additional open green space in future phases of the housing community. A win-win for all. Thank you."

When she hadn't choked on her words or peed her pants, a sudden release of adrenaline surged through her young body. Her rubbery legs somehow hadn't given out. The overwhelming sense of accomplishment was real.

Had anyone listened?

Brooke Lynn had been unaware of the classroom's silence while she spoke. She caught Todd's wink. Well, at least *he* had been listening.

"Well-prepared and nicely put together," Miss Hart murmured.

Brooke Lynn hoped for a top grade. She smiled back at Todd.

Is winking flirting?

Out in the hallway, Todd tapped her arm, motioning her to the side.

"Hey there, Brooke Lynn. Way to go on your speech. Since I hadn't talked to my uncle in a couple of days, I learned a lot about what had finally been decided about the trails. You know, my dad asked me if I knew who you were after you left the note about the speeder."

"Your dad?" Brooke Lynn was amazed. She'd had no idea the site manager was his father. "Your dad is Joe, the construction manager?"

"Yeah," Todd nodded. "He wants to meet you to thank you. Stop by his trailer when you can. I told him we were just getting to know each other but I knew that you liked to hike. Um, we should go sometime," Todd offered.

"That would be great! Thanks, Todd. So, your dad is the construction manager, Joe, who left me the message. Aah. Do you know who's moving into the first home?" Brooke Lynn asked.

"No, I've tried to overhear, but they've been so secretive about who it is that I gave up," he said.

"Huh! Wonder what's the big deal… oh well. And yeah, I'd like to go hiking sometime. The company would be nice," Brooke Lynn confirmed, feeling her cheeks flush slightly.

"We'll have to wait until after the opening party. I have to help my dad and uncle out at the site until then," Todd said.

"That works for me. Thanks again for listening to my speech. Okay, see you later."

Wondering where her two buddies were hanging out today at lunch, Brooke Lynn picked a table by the back. She could see the whole cafeteria facing the food line. Neither one walked in. Were they hanging out together? Wiggling in her seat, she looked up every time a classmate passed by. Thinking back to her conversation with Todd, she longed to tell Susie about the fact he'd asked her hiking. And Mike… well, she was starting to miss him. Darn phone restriction!

A sadness swept over her about their changing relationships. Was she ready to deal with her friendship challenges and pass the note on to Susie? No, not yet. She walked back to class alone, cutting her lunch break short.

Brooke Lynn didn't see her besties for the rest of the week. Instead, she spent time with two of her new classmates, Todd and Rachel, during their lunch breaks. Susie's note sat in her bookbag like an irritating rash. She couldn't keep ignoring it. She missed them a lot!

The rumors about the supposed new owners went into overdrive by Friday. Brooke Lynn couldn't believe the various versions circling the school. Because of these so-called celebrity sightings, it was rowdier in the classroom than normal. No more mention about the injured celebrity… was any of it true? Well, the mysterious man with Mr. Clemens was real. Doubt set in Brooke Lynn's mind regarding her ability to figure it out. Her intuitive sixth sense wasn't paying off like it had in previous investigations.

"Everyone, time to settle down. Rachel, Todd, get back in your seats. Okay, it's taken me all week to review your papers. Overall, everyone surpassed my expectations," Miss Hart smiled.

Brooke Lynn Gale shifted in her chair. She watched the pile being passed down her aisle. When the stack landed on her desk, she hesitated to look. She opened one eye, then both, and shrieked.

"Eek, I got an A+!!"

She had said it too loudly. Miss Hart glared, shaking her head. Brooke Lynn's knees buckled as she settled back in her seat. The class chatter held an excitable level until the bell rang for lunchtime. She decided she liked this result *much* better than the C+ from the science test!

Today was the day to give Susie her note no matter what! Brooke Lynn walked in earnest to the cafeteria to locate Mike or Susie. She wanted to talk to Mike about their friendship too. They had stuff to catch up on. With the weekend ahead, it was making her crazy.

Mike caught sight of Brooke Lynn first. He tossed his essay across the table, pointing to the grade. She looked up and grinned at his happiness. It was good to see him.

"B+, wow, buddy, maybe Susie's tutoring paid off," Brooke Lynn noted.

Mike then pointed to the personal note from Mr. Clemens on his paper. He was smiling as Brooke Lynn read the note out loud.

"Mike, the class thoroughly enjoyed you being open and honest while sharing your story about your dad. Well done, Mr. C."

Brooke Lynn gleamed at the sight of her bestie. His chest was so puffed out, she thought it might split open.

"Awesome, Mike! I did well too. Hey not to switch the subject but tell me what happened after your dad dropped me off on Saturday. Then I'll fill you in on me."

Brooke Lynn had missed him and it had only been six days! She wished her emotions towards him weren't so baffling. Mike grew serious.

"Where have you been hanging out? I looked for you a few times but never saw you. Were you avoiding me?"

"Well, yeah, kind of. I knew I had a few things on my mind and wanted to talk to you… but I wasn't quite ready. But today seemed like a good enough time," Brooke Lynn dared say.

"Okay, I guess. To be honest, I've been keeping to myself all week too. It was harsh, BL. My dad was ticked off. He said I was grounded for one week with no phone privileges or any outside activities, except for school."

Brooke Lynn nodded in understanding, and was ready to continue, when Susie bopped over to join in.

Susie was smirking while handing her essay over. Brooke Lynn scanned the comments on her paper and read them out loud too.

"A-, a well-deserved grade," Brooke Lynn recited. "You were poised and confident in your delivery. Nice job, Susie. Mr. C."

"Yeah, I'm excited about it. He said I got the minus instead of the A+ because I misspelled some words. Darn," Susiee replied.

"That's great. Congratulations, Susie. And it's so good to see you. Sorry I haven't been around but I wasn't ready to talk to you earlier in the week. I've had a lot on my mind. I guess I was, um, well, I'm ready now," Brooke Lynn said.

Her hand quivered as she pulled out the envelope from the inside pocket of her bookbag. Brooke Lynn's eye twitched. Almost dropping it, she snatched it just in time by the crumpled edge. With a regrip, she handed it over to Susie.

"I really want to talk to you if that's okay – it's important. It's kind of personal. Do you mind taking a sec to read it now?" Brooke Lynn asked.

"Okay, but let's talk over at another table. More private," Susie responded.

"Sure. Back in a bit, Mike," Brooke Lynn said.

She hoped Susie wanted to talk first. Brooke Lynn wondered if she'd gone too far. Maybe their friendship was beyond repair. The tick in her eye returned.

Chapter Thirty-One

SUSIE REYNOLDS TALKS

Susie finished reading and without hesitation, bit right into Brooke Lynn.

"Yeah, Mike told me already that he was grounded because of the little caper you two went on. So, I kind of figured you were also grounded when I didn't hear from you. I saw you Tuesday in the hallway but you looked like you were going through something. I wasn't sure so, I waved instead. I was surprised when you didn't come around all week. You know, I thought we were better friends than that!"

While Susie gathered her thoughts, Brooke Lynn grew more anxious and adjusted in her seat. Susie continued.

"You don't need to worry about Mike and me. I think of him as a brother. To be honest, he's not my type anyway. So, get off that thought, okay? Is that why you've been so testy lately? Well, let it go because there's nothing there!"

Susie fumed, letting that sink in before starting again.

"And anyway, I have someone I'm interested in. I haven't had a chance to tell you yet. So, Todd from your class, well, I've been waiting for some sort of signal from him. I think he's so cute. We've been kind of flirting with each other like when I see him in the hallway. And yesterday, he was waiting for me by my locker. He seems cool. What do you think of him?" Susie cooed.

Brooke Lynn let out a sigh of relief. Her friend wasn't as mad as she had feared, but she was worried that there could be another boy-related incident what with Todd having invited *h*er hiking!

"For some reason, I was so afraid to ask you about Mike. I think that's why I avoided giving you the note all week. I thought you'd be offended. I guess I was kind of jealous that Mike came to you for tutoring instead of me. Sometimes I'm over-protective and a bit selfish with my friendships, including you too. We've been through a lot together, Susie. Just so you know, I've been avoiding Mike too because I have such strange, mixed emotions about him. It was easier to not talk about it. But I'm so glad we're talking now, Susie. It's a big relief. Well, enough of that… tell me more about you and Todd. So, you like him, huh?"

As they sat there talking like old times, Brooke Lynn was grateful she and Susie were making up. She hoped they would be okay. Her fingers were crossed under the table.

"Yeah, he seems like a neat guy. We'll see what happens, but I can't wait until school each day to see him. So, I guess that means I've got a crush on him. Don't tell anyone, okay?" Susie confided.

"I promise I won't say a word to anyone about you and Todd until you're ready. I should tell you that he's invited me hiking at some point, but I'm guessing it's either as just friends or as a way to get to know you maybe?" Brooke Lynn asked, wondering if Todd's friendliness was just his attempt to get closer to Susie.

"I don't like him in that way so don't worry. I feel so much better, Susie. I don't want anything to come between our friendship, especially boys. I thought for sure you were hung up on Mike. My friendship with Mike has been on again, off again so much since the summer. It's been driving me nuts. I'm just excited you and I are good," Brooke Lynn finished.

"Let's not let anything ruin our friendship, and I agree, especially boys! G-i-r-l-s… rock!" Susie exclaimed.

Susie got up to give Brooke Lynn a hug. The embrace was returned, confirming their solid friendship.

"Hey, Susie, there he is over there… Todd, and he's looking back over here. See him?" Brooke Lynn asked.

She wanted to point but held back. She remembered her promise.

"Eek, that's him… don't look. Stop looking! I don't want him to see me staring at him. He asked to come over to my house after school to hang out sometime. I told him I'd have to ask my mother if it's okay first. But I think I really like him. My mother says I can't start dating until I'm at least a sophomore in high school. That's over two years away which is forever! I hate being a kid sometimes," her friend fussed.

"Um, about the dating thing, I haven't given it a whole lot of thought. I'm sure it'll happen soon enough," Brooke Lynn replied.

Brooke Lynn felt boy-crazy, but she didn't feel ready beyond friendship with any of them. There was something about Mike though… Brooke Lynn just hadn't sorted it out.

"Well, I'm heading back to class. See you tomorrow," Susie said.

Waving bye to Susie, she watched her friend saunter over to Todd. She looked on, proud of her friend for having such confidence. Brooke Lynn hoped in time she'd feel more self-assured and gain more courage.

She turned her attention to her other bestie, Mike, sitting by himself. Did she see Mike's expression fall when Susie left? Maybe she had it all wrong. Was *Mike* into Susie?

Brooke Lynn blinked a few times in alarming disbelief. His face didn't look happy at all.

Chapter Thirty-Two

ASK MIKE

"Hey, what's with the sad face? Let me guess... your dad or someone else? I've been beside myself too but mainly because I miss having my phone. It would have come in handy to stay in touch with you and Susie this week. Speaking of Susie, something's bugging me so, I'm just going to say it. I was wondering... do you like Susie?" Brooke Lynn asked.

"Say, what? Susie? As in like-like? *Geez,* BL!" Mike said shocked, almost choking.

"Well, I saw you staring at her when she first walked over to us. And then when she just left, you looked sad. Was I imagining it?"

Feeling awkward much?

She blurted it out before stopping herself. Her face blushed when Mike shook his head.

"What an imagination, BL! No! I am not interested in Susie or any girls for that matter. Get off it! I've been too busy concentrating on schoolwork and trying to make things right with my dad. It crushed me, Brooke Lynn." Mike cleared his throat.

I've really messed up now!

"No, I was probably just staring off into space. I'm just upset at myself for letting my dad down. It's the worst feeling. I just can't wrap my head around how I thought it was even remotely smart. What was I thinking? What about you?" Mike asked glumly.

Brooke Lynn was glad she was talking to Mike after days of dodging him. It felt good to air her grief even if he was annoyed with her.

"Sorry I've been avoiding you, Mike. But this whole restriction thing has been messing with me. Luckily, my dad has been working long hours lately, so he's been quiet about the whole thing. My mom, well, we've had some arguments, small stuff mostly, but still squabbles. I can sort of see where she's coming from. It's just so frustrating sometimes. Anyway, tackling my to-do list and helping my mom keeps me busy. I organized my bedroom and closet. Looks cool. Oh, we planted some geraniums in the flower beds. She showed me how to compost. That's her thing – the gardening. But it beats being bored. The hardest part was no phone."

She was intentionally trying to switch the subject from her earlier comments. That restless feeling returned. The pencil she was twirling between her fingers fell onto the shiny lunch table. It rolled to the other side. She left it alone, placing her hands under her thighs.

Should I ask?

"Hey, on another subject, want to go with me to the party tomorrow? We won't be grounded any longer, so it'll be the first fun thing we get to do once our restriction is lifted. My folks are probably going with your parents. I was hoping you'd want to ride bikes over, that way we can leave whenever we want. Plus, we need to close *The Case of the Hidden Shoe. Who* is the mysterious homeowner that Mr. Clemens has kept from everyone? And there'll be live music with tons of food and free ice cream. Maybe meet a celeb or two? What do you say?" Brooke Lynn asked.

Ugh, should I have waited until he asked me instead?

"Um, okay yeah. You're always thinking, BL. What's the big secret of who's moving in anyway? So weird! Hard to believe no one knows. Kind of tired of everyone talking about it too. The case is almost closed anyway now we know the shoe belongs to my dad."

"The case can't be closed until we know who the client is!" Brooke Lynn declared.

"I know, you're right," Mike agreed. "I'll be glad when we can close the case with the name of the mysterious client. And I agree, it's tough getting stuck when the folks don't want to leave. So, my dad has me cleaning out the garage with him a little each day. Part of my punishment, I guess. At least I'm spending time with him. Crazy year, BL," Mike answered.

Brooke Lynn sighed in agreement.

"Yeah, still wondering why your dad met Mr. Clemens at the house in the first place? Visiting an old friend because he hadn't seen him in a while and getting school updates on you? I don't know. The whole Mr. Clemens thing has been strange. It sure has been a tough week filled with good and bad stuff," she said perplexed.

"BL, my dad is so stoked to be home. But he's *still* looking for a job. He seems worried. Like the job could be out-of-state," Mike said.

"Well, I don't want you to move either. Think positive. He'll find something nearby soon," Brooke Lynn said.

A small gasp escaped. She couldn't imagine what she'd do if Mike moved far away.

The bell rang two short tones, signaling lunch period was over. Brooke Lynn was disappointed it was the end of their break. She was enjoying their conversation.

"Mike, about what I asked earlier – you know, about Susie - I'm still trying to figure things out too. It's all confusing. I wonder what it will be like when you get a girlfriend some day and I get a boyfriend? Do you think we'll still be friends?" she asked concerned.

"I'm sure we will. I don't think about that kind of stuff, BL. It happens when it happens, I guess," he replied.

For a moment, Brooke Lynn allowed to imagine what it would feel like to be his girlfriend. Was she feeling a bit rejected he didn't seem into her? What a silly idea… she snapped out of it.

"See you tomorrow, pal," Brooke Lynn said.

She gave Mr. Clemens' hushed conversations with a mystery client some more thought. Brooke Lynn couldn't quite put her finger on it. Was it one of their mutual friends? A celebrity? Or another teacher like Mr. Colby? This case was the first one that had stumped her. They'd figured out the hidden shoe mystery but couldn't quite distinguish who the low-voiced client was… yet. She'd keep on it until the party.

Why am I overly excited about tomorrow?

Chapter Thirty-Three

GRAND OPENING PARTY

The event day had finally arrived, it had been a long week.

"Hey, Mom, now that my restriction is lifted, am I allowed to have phone privileges again?" Brooke Lynn asked early over breakfast.

"Oh, actually, your grounding isn't over until later this afternoon, but I think it's been long enough. Your father and I noticed how you stepped up your responsibilities around the house, along with your schoolwork. Also, getting along with your brother has been nice. Although you made a poor choice last weekend, you seem sorry about your actions. Let's hope we don't have to go through that again," her mom stated.

"Thanks, Mom. I didn't think about how you or Dad would feel. I'm glad it's over," Brooke Lynn said.

She couldn't wait to text Mike and Susie.

"SWL ☺ BK ON, WAN2TLKL."

She got a thumbs up and smiley emoji back from both.

After getting her homework and household tasks done, she sprawled out on her partially made bed. Admiring her spiffy updated bedroom, she stuffed the over-sized pillow behind her. Propped up, she phoned Susie. It felt great catching up with her girlfriend. They laughed and chatted about pretty much everything and nothing, just like one of their lazy sleepovers.

"Hey, are you going with Todd to the party?" Brooke Lynn asked.

"Todd's meeting me there. I asked if he knew who the new homeowners were and if they were from Hollywood. He said his dad and uncle are being tight-lipped about it. Keeping it a secret at the request of the client. So, until we get to the party it's anyone's guess. I hope they're movie stars."

When Brooke Lynn hung up she scanned her closet. She pulled out one of the latest outfits Susie had helped her pick out. Taking extra time to get changed, Brooke Lynn admired how the navy-blue cropped pants fit on her hips.

She put on the new lime green camp shirt paired with her slacks. Fun top, but it seemed a little boxy over the bottoms. Still unsure, she tossed it aside and tried on the pink V-neck T-shirt. In her opinion, the combination layered better with the blue-and-white striped cardigan. She'd need the sweater when it cooled off later.

Opting to wear her hair down with her mother's silver barrette, her reflection displayed a more grownup version of herself. She turned sideways noting how long her hair had grown. She slowly swished her hair, letting the front locks cascade behind her shoulders. Pleased with the outcome, she headed out to the party texting as she walked.

"3, R U RDY?" she asked.

"C U N 10," Mike replied.

A bunch of people were milling around the party's arched front entrance when they turned into the gated compound. They parked in the designated bike stand. Hearing the loud chatter made it clear the party was well-underway. The white, gold and silver balloons tethered high above the tables darted side-to-side in the breezy fall air. It was the biggest event since last year's annual Christmas tree lighting.

A Country-Western band could be heard playing an upbeat twang of a tune. With boots stomping and hands clapping to the beat, they watched the couples twirling together on the dance floor. Brooke Lynn nudged Mike, pointing to their folks doing the two-step.

They meandered around until they came upon some children getting their chubby faces painted by one of the local artists. The giggling kids made them snicker. With the smoky scent of barbecue wafting across the crowd, it triggered their hunger.

"Our parents are having a good time. Look at 'em. And, m-m-m, it smells so good," Mike confirmed.

"What a buzzing crowd. Gosh, I love it. Yeah, let's eat," Brooke Lynn agreed.

When Mike looked back at his bestie, a nagging thought crossed his mind. His pal was wearing her hair down for a change with a glittery barrette. When had she gotten those cute freckles across her nose? With a degree of shyness, he turned away.

"Let's go look at the 3-D model of the site over there first and then get some grub," he blurted out.

They squirmed through the crowd by the display table, then steered their way to the multi-tiered banquet tables loaded with various salads, finger sandwiches, chips and dips, plus an array of desserts. With a mountain of delicious munchies, they loaded up their plates.

While they munched away and viewed the site, Brooke Lynn realized she was in full sensory overload. The featured home prominently stood out against the unfinished structures of the site. Exterior lighting emphasized its grandness. It looked right out of a home and garden magazine.

"You'd never know it was a messy construction site a few days ago. Everything is so clean and swept. Hey, we better grab our free ice cream before any speeches and the line gets too long," Brooke Lynn said. "Hi, Mrs. Hardiman, hi Ceci, isn't this so fun? Have you heard any scoop about the lucky new owners?"

"Hi, guys," the owner of the ice cream stall greeted them. "I think it has to be an outsider. Rita saw some movie star coming out of the clinic with a bandage of some kind. What would he be doing here if he wasn't looking at the homes? We keep looking around the crowd for a celebrity but nothing yet. I can't wait to see who it is."

People were trying to jockey for a good position in front of the stage. Standing up by the microphone was Mayor Douglas, the developer, Mr. Smythe and Mr. Clemens.

"Hey, look at Mr. Clemens up there. I guess we are finally going to see who his client is any minute. Oh, by the way, I checked online about the airline stub info and SFO stands for San Francisco airport. So maybe the new homeowner is from up north?" Brooke Lynn said.

"Not sure. I kind of hope it's someone famous. Be so cool. I just know that the lucky homeowner is getting a nice place. You and I both liked it."

"Well, we're about to find out. Then we can close the case," Brooke Lynn replied.

Mr. Larkin was talking with Mr. Clemens near the podium, probably catching up on old times. Brooke Lynn wondered again what Mr. Larkin had said about Mr. Clemens - something about them working together overseas years ago and emails about Mike.

"Mike, I guess Mr. Clemens and your dad are pretty close friends. He's all chummy with him. Look," Brooke Lynn observed.

"Yeah, he said he knew him from work and stuff, but I never met him before he was my teacher," Mike responded.

Brooke Lynn peeked at her watch – 4:00. As Mayor Douglas and Mr. Smythe shared the microphone explaining the project, she scanned the crowd looking for Susie. Going on longer than she'd like, she almost missed the start of Mr. Clemens' speech.

"Ladies and gentlemen, neighbors, friends, and family, it has been a pleasure working with the developer, Mr. Smythe, on the very first home of Phase I. On behalf of my client's request, I have kept the new owner's identity confidential. Most of you know me as a teacher at the middle school, but occasionally I dabble in real estate for select clients. Today, the secret will be revealed. But first, is everyone having a great time, so far? Smythe Development knows how to throw a party, right?" Mr. Clemens asked.

The applause went on for quite some time. It was a rowdy crowd.

"But, please, please, settle down. Prior to announcing the new homeowners of the stunning showcase home, my longtime friend, Ernie Larkin, has a special request. Afterwards, I promise… we'll get to the announcement. Ernie, come on over."

Brooke Lynn watched her friend's dad step up and take the microphone. She wondered what his request was.

"Hi, everyone, I'd like to get my son up here. Test. Can you hear me? Test, test… one, two, um," Mr. Larkin said.

As he fumbled with the microphone, his voice faded out. Brooke Lynn listened closely and then she knew what he was going to say. It struck Brooke Lynn like a ton of bricks. O-M-Goodness!

Chapter Thirty-Four

SURPRISE CLIENT

"Mike, remember when you thought you heard your dad's…" Brooke Lynn's words hung in the air.

"What?" Mike asked.

Mr. Clemens approached the podium, switched a button and, after an ear-piercing audio squeal, the microphone was working again. He gave it a tap and nodded to Mr. Larkin.

"Can everyone hear? Okay, first, um, Mike, come on up, come up here, stand next to your mother, please. I want to say a few words," his dad said more clearly.

She watched Mike and his mother step onto the stage with a silly look embedded on his face. Could it be what she was thinking? Had she been too close to the family to fully get it? It all made sense to her now.

Brooke Lynn's mind raced. The large speaker she was standing next to echoed with Mr. Larkin's words. No longer low and hushed, the mysterious voice was recognizable at last.

"Mike, I know it's been difficult as a family with me working overseas, but I knew one day I'd be back home for good. There was always an end game, son, to that sacrifice. Thank you both for your love and strength over the years. It truly kept me going. So, Mike and Annie, I have a *big* surprise for you today," Mr. Larkin said, then stepped away from the podium.

He turned toward Mr. Clemens and gave a short nod. Still unsure where this was going, Mike didn't dare move.

"Mr. Smythe, please do the honors," Mr. Clemens requested.

When Mr. Smythe walked across the stage, he shook Mr. Larkin's hand. Then he placed something in Mr. Larkin's palm. A murmur started through the crowd as Mr. Smythe faced the townspeople.

"On behalf of Oak Grove Homes, and without further ado, I'd like to present to you the *first* homeowners - The Larkin Family! Welcome, and may you live a long, healthy, and happy life in your brand-new home. Everyone... The Larkins."

The crowd erupted into a roaring applause and hollering. Annie Larkin wept uncontrollably. She covered her face with her hands, unable to look back up at her smiling husband.

Mike stood still, shocked by what was transpiring. Brooke Lynn ran up to her buddy and gave him a hug. She pulled Mike toward their folks by his lifeless arm.

"Congratulations, my friends. Oh, my goodness!" The Gales shouted.

Mr. Gale shoved his shoulder toward Mr. Larkin in a friendly push and embrace.

"You rascal, Ernie, I can't believe you kept this from me. First your military retirement and now this! We've got some chatting to do, pal," Mick Gale said.

"Yes, we do, and I look forward to that long chat with you, Mick. Keeping it hush-hush from Annie, Mike, you, well, darn near everyone... it was harder than I thought. But I'll fill you in over a cold one later," Mr. Larkin teased.

"When Ernie took the keys from Mr. Smythe, I cried like a baby, you guys!" Annie Larkin squealed. "I can't believe he was able to keep this a secret from me and Mike. I didn't think he even *liked* the new development based on how he talked down about it. He sure fooled us all! Oh, Sally, girlfriend, I have no words. First, him retiring, then a new job and now this! And to think our kids nearly caught him by sneaking over here the other night!"

"Hey, you okay, buddy?" Brooke Lynn asked Mike, noticing he still looked shocked.

"Yeah, it's foggy, but finally registering. Unbelievable," he answered.

"I figured it out, Mike. The clues were all there. Seeing your dad up there, talking low, trying to get the mic to work, *he* was the hushed voice. We never asked your dad the most important question that night at the new house; *why* was he visiting Mr. Clemens there? Was he visiting as an old friend and your teacher, or… as the new homeowner? *He* was Mr. Clemens' secret client all along."

Mike was piecing the clues together in his fuzzy state.

"So, I wasn't overly tired, it *was* his voice I thought I recognized! And the ticket stub was probably his too, not some celebrity. Now that I think about it, my dad talked about some of his overseas flights connecting through San Francisco… SFO. We were both so scared when my dad caught us at the house, we forgot our own detective questions, BL. Being on restriction, well, we didn't get a chance to put our heads together."

"Yeah, and about the celebrity Susie's mom supposedly saw coming out of the clinic, it sounds more likely that it was a case of mistaken identity. Don't you agree?" Brooke Lynn asked, but before Mike could answer, another announcement came over the PA system. Brooke Lynn and Mike smiled listening to his dad's voice. It was *very* clear now.

"Thank you again for coming to the grand opening party. I know you were waiting for some celebrity to show up. Sorry about that, but I feel like a rock star just being back home with you all. Now everyone is invited to walk through our new home as soon as I test out these shiny new keys," Mr. Larkin said.

He held the brass keyring high. Mike looked up at his dad and truly saw a different man. He had kept his promise and then some.

As soon as they entered the home, the themed feature wall in the family room hit the two crime-stoppers between the eyes. The paint color was **cranberry red**. Brooke Lynn and Mike smiled at each other knowingly. The infamous spilled paint can had set the investigation in motion.

Brooke Lynn thought no one else needed to know about the spilled red paint, the so-called mystery of the hidden shoe and questioning Mr. Clemens' motives. He wasn't devious at all - just helping an old friend. And through it all, her pal had his dad home for good. And so, did she – there was no risk of him moving to a different state. All the details of the mystery would be left in the case file and only shared between the two of them.

While they people-watched, it felt like old times with her bestie. For the first time in weeks, Brooke Lynn felt comfortable in her own skin standing next to Mike.

"So, I guess this means my pal isn't moving away?" Brooke Lynn teased.

"Nope, my dad told Mom and me last night that he got a new job and it starts right away. Get this, it's at your dad's company - just like you said. I still can't believe he's home for good. Funny part is, after worrying about having to move away, well, I *am* moving... just in the same neighborhood!" Mike laughed.

CHAPTER THIRTY-FIVE

IT'S A WRAP!

"I'm glad you're not moving away, Mike. And I'm sure my dad is super excited having his best friend home *and* working together in the cyber security firm. Cyber hackers beware of that duo. Hey, there she is! Geez. Was wondering where Susie was," Brooke Lynn said.

Susie was directly across the room from them. Standing next to her was Todd, her new crush. Brooke Lynn could tell by her friend's expression she seemed happy. They were engaged in a conversation with an older man. She smiled and waved at her girlfriend.

"Todd and I are planning a hike soon. Maybe I can talk Susie into coming. You can join us too. He seems like a neat guy," Brooke Lynn stated.

"Oh? I don't know him. Hiking, huh," Mike answered.

Is there a hint of jealousy from Mike?

A few steps away was Susie's mother talking with Mr. Clemens. Brooke Lynn thought they looked cute together. She nudged Mike.

"See that man talking to Susie and Todd? He's keeps looking over at us. Wonder who he could be? Oh no, Mike, he caught me looking at him, and now he's motioning for us to come over. Guess we better go over," Brooke Lynn said, lightly pushing Mike.

"Hi there, I'm Joe Smythe the construction manager, the one who left you the message. It's nice to finally meet you in person, Brooke Lynn. And, congratulations, Mike, on being the first family to move into Oak Grove Homes. We're proud how the home turned out," Joe said.

"It's nice to meet you too. So, you're Todd's father, Mr. Smythe, right? Hi, Todd, hi Susie," Brooke Lynn said.

"Yeah, that's my boy. He's a good kid. Anyway, I wanted to thank you personally for leaving the note at my trailer. Several other neighbors had complained about a speeding truck but based on your detailed description, we knew who the employee was at last. He was not happy about being let go, but we're hoping that's the last of him. I don't think there's been any trouble since, right?" Joe added.

"No, sir, haven't seen any speeders, been quiet." Brooke Lynn shook her head.

"Let me know if anything else comes up and keep up the good work. What did Mr. Wilkens call you? Oh yeah, *2-K Team*. Thank you both again and enjoy the party," Joe said.

Without trying to appear too prideful, Brooke Lynn and Mike turned their attention to their folks.

"Congratulations, Mr. and Mrs. Larkin. I'm glad you don't have to move away; it wouldn't be the same without you all. And Mom, Dad, did you have *any* idea?" Brooke Lynn asked.

"Honey, we were as surprised as everyone. Ernie pulled it off all on his own, well, with the help of Tim, ah, Mr. Clemens I mean," her dad exclaimed.

"I have to tell you, Brooke Lynn, when I saw you and Mike at the new house, I was disappointed you both had snuck out. That part was true," Mike's dad said. "But I also got a bit nervous; I thought you had guessed I was there on business… homeowner business. I'm relieved Joe finished the build in time, it was getting harder to keep it under wraps with everyone talking about it. It was important for it to be a complete surprise to my family. That's why Mr. Clemens had to keep it a secret. But I had no idea it would turn into the town gossip though. Geez," Ernie Larkin confessed.

They all chuckled at him pulling off the caper.

"Hey Dad, can I choose which bedroom will be mine?"

"Sure Mike, what room were you thinking?" his dad asked.

"I know exactly - the last bedroom on the right. It's got a perfect view of the back yard right where my soccer practice net is going." Mike grinned.

"Well, you sure did keep it a secret, Mr. Larkin. Even the *2-K Team* had trouble with this one. We didn't think you liked the project so it threw us off. Very clever. Oh, Mom, I haven't seen Arnie. Is he here?" Brooke Lynn asked.

"No, Belinda had to babysit so he volunteered to keep her company. I think he really likes her," her mother answered.

Brooke Lynn's shoulders sagged a little, she had been hoping to finally meet the person who was taking up all her brother's thoughts.

"Hey, Brooke Lynn, what about one more ice cream?" Mike interrupted her pondering.

Brooke Lynn wondered what caught Mike's interest as they walked toward the vendor's stand. She followed his gaze to the backs of Mrs. Hardiman and Todd straight across.

Was there a snare underneath her buddy's glare?

Brooke Lynn hoped that one day Mike and Todd could be good friends, maybe even meet up for a hike.

Licking the creamy strawberry drip from the end of her cone, she looked at Mike and giggled. He had a wide chocolate ring around his mouth. She decided not to tease him since they were in a good place. She wished everything would stay this way forever.

When she and Mike rode home, a pesky lump lodged in her throat. She couldn't gulp it away with a hard swallow. She needed to talk to Susie!

"Oh good, you picked up. You know how you asked if I liked Mike you know, had feelings for him?" Brooke Lynn stated breathlessly.

"Yeah, so have you figured it out yet? Do *you* like Mike?" Susie asked.

"Well, it's been on my mind ever since you asked. I'm still a bit mixed up about how I feel. But… um, yeah, I do like him and *more* than just a friend. I think the threat of him potentially moving away and then the relief of knowing he won't need to move, made me realize how much I like him. Don't say anything to anyone though until I understand it more, okay?"

Brooke Lynn smiled now that she had shared her secret with Susie. Their sister bond was tightly secured.

"Of course. Besties forever! See you Monday!" Susie replied.

All tucked in for the evening, Brooke Lynn opened her iPad. She clicked on the file folder of *The Case of the Hidden Shoe*, added a final sleuth note, then marked it – **Case Closed**.

Her mind replayed the events of the day. She couldn't believe how happy everyone was, it had been wonderful to spend the day with her family and…

Wait, Arnie wasn't there, he was with his girlfriend who he keeps promising we'll meet. Why hasn't he let us meet Belinda yet? Is he hiding something?

Brooke Lynn shrugged the questions away; it had been a long day and she was tired. She finally closed the screen.

Reaching for the lamp, she saw the blue blinking light on her phone. It was from Mike.

"Need to talk ASAP! New Case!"

About the Author...

Toby A. Williams made her debut as a published children's book author in December 2018. The five-book rhyming series, *The BROOKE LYNN Adventures* has won several prominent children's picture book awards, along with recognition from the Local Author Spotlight programs of the San Diego Public Library and Barnes & Nobel.

Her latest work, *The BROOKE LYNN Mysteries*, a middle-grade fiction series, has been an exhilarating experience on her writing journey. She resides in the San Diego area of Southern California.

"Brooke Lynn has inspired many early readers over the years. This was a perfect sequel to the rhyming stories. And like her fans, I wanted to see her blossom into a thriving pre-teen youngster. It has been a thrill to relive those earlier years through the eyes of Brooke Lynn," reflected Author Williams.

Visit her on Facebook, Instagram, and Author Website, **www.tobyawilliamsauthor.com**

#thebrookelynnadventuresandmysteries
@thebrookelynnadventures

If you liked this story, please consider leaving an honest Review by visiting the Author's Pages below and clicking on the book link. Reviews are a terrific way to compliment the author and give valuable insight. Please take a moment now that you've read The Case of the Hidden Shoe. Thank you… your Review is appreciated.

https://www.amazon.com/author/tobywilliams
or
https://www.tobyawilliamsauthor.com

Made in the USA
Middletown, DE
12 July 2021